The Bloody Score

Bolan smiled and began speaking: "We all know the score. Now let's talk about operations. Today's soft probe was a success from every angle. Giordano was my only sure link with the western branch of the family. Now he knows we're in town. He knows we're on to him. We killed two of his boys, we wrecked his house, we took a chunk of money away from him, we humiliated him, and we showed him that he is living strictly at our pleasure. That's a helluva bitter mouthful for a Mafia honcho to chew on. He'll be laying quiet for a few hours, at least until the cops stop poking around the neighborhood. Then he'll start flexing his muscles and demanding our heads on a Mafia platter. This is precisely what we want him to do. We're playing a Vanh Duc game here guys," Bolan explained. "Only there will be no air force or infantry reinforcements to finish the job once we've smoked the enemy into the open. We have to do the entire job ourselves. We're going to hit 'em, and hit 'em, and keep on hitting 'em until they're trying to hide up each other's asses. Then, when we know who they are and where they are, all of them—then we squash them. That's the entire plan."

The Executioner Series:

the EXECUTIONER
DEATH SQUAD

by Don Pendleton

PINNACLE BOOKS   NEW YORK

EXECUTIONER #2: DEATH SQUAD

Copyright © 1969 by Pinnacle Books, Inc.

An original Pinnacle Books edition, published for the first time anywhere.

ISBN: 0-523-41714-4

First printing, September, 1969
Second printing, April, 1970
Third printing, October, 1970
Fourth printing, April, 1971
Fifth printing, June, 1971
Sixth printing, December, 1971
Seventh printing, June, 1972
Eighth printing, July, 1972
Ninth printing, November, 1972
Tenth printing, March, 1974
Eleventh printing, September, 1975
Twelfth printing, November, 1976
Thirteenth printing, October, 1977
Fourteenth printing, April, 1978
Fifteenth printing, June, 1978
Sixteenth printing, December, 1978
Seventeenth printing, July, 1979
Eighteenth printing, October, 1979
Nineteenth printing, July, 1980
Twentieth printing, January, 1981
Twenty-first printing, December, 1981
Twenty-second printing, May, 1982

Cover illustration by Gil Cohen

Printed in the United States of America

PINNACLE BOOKS, INC.
1430 Broadway
New York, New York 10018

DEDICATION

For my sergeant son, Steve—and for all those gallant men of the Long Range Reconnaissance Patrols,
9th Infantry Division, Vietnam.

But wherefore thou alone? Wherefore with thee
Came not *all hell broke loose?*
> —John Milton, *Paradise Lost*

We'll hit the Mafia so fast, so often, and from
so many directions they'll think hell fell on them.
We steal, we kill, we terrorize, and we take
every Goddamned thing they have. Then we'll
see how powerful and well organized they are.
> —Mack Bolan, THE EXECUTIONER

DEATH SQUAD

PROLOGUE

Of all the grim specialties developed by U.S. fighting men in Vietnam, Mack Bolan had fallen heir to the most ruthless and cold-blooded job of all. Sergeant Bolan was a sharpshooter, a nerveless perfectionist, and a man who could certainly command himself. He quickly became the most renowned sniper of the combat zones. His many kills and daring methodology had earned for him the unofficial title of The Executioner. And then Mack Bolan had been summoned home on an emergency furlough to bury his father, his mother, and his teenage sister—victims of violent death. Bolan learned that the international crime syndicate known as the Mafia had indirectly figured into the tragedies.

Bolan's grief turned to white-hot fury, and he declared all-out warfare on the local Mafia entrenchments of his hometown, the Eastern city of Pittsfield. Unhampered by the usual restrictions imposed on legal authorities, Bolan carried jungle-warfare concepts directly to the enemy, and The Executioner's Battle of Pittsfield became an American legend overnight. Single handedly he smoked out the gangland principals and executed them in a daring series of encounters. "I am not their judge," Bolan declared. "I am their judgment—I am their executioner!"

But he was definitely outside the law. Though many officials secretly applauded the executioner's actions, he was officially charged with multiple counts of murder, arson, intimidation, and miscellaneous mayhem. And to the executioner's certain

1

knowledge, he had found no victory at Pittsfield. He had become a man marked for death, sought by every law-enforcement agency in the nation and with every resource of the worldwide Mafia organization geared to his destruction. Bolan left Pittsfield with the feeling that he was setting out on his last mile—but he was determined to stretch that final mile to its highest yield, to fight the war to its last gasp. Mack Bolan's last mile was going to be a bloody one. The Executioner would live life to the very end.

Chapter One

THE GAME

The Executioner arrived in Los Angeles on the evening of September 20 without fanfare or prior announcement. Approaching from Las Vegas, he followed the freeways across the city, exited into Santa Monica, and angled southward along the coastal highway. Several minutes later he pulled alongside a telephone booth at a service station, consulted the directory, then thumbed a dime into the coinbox and dialed the number of an ex army buddy, Vietnam veteran George Zitka. A cautious voice answered the ring. Bolan grinned and spoke crisply into the mouthpiece. "Early Bird, this is Fireman. What is your situation there?"

A startled gasp, then momentary silence. Then a voice of quiet emotion replied, "Situation normal, Fireman. Suggest you bypass and proceed direct to Kwang Tri."

"Negative," Bolan replied, his voice stiffening somewhat. "It's time for R and R, and I'm coming in."

"Suggest Kwang Tri for R and R," the voice responded in controlled urgency.

"Negative, I'm coming in," Bolan clipped. He hung up, stared thoughtfully at the dial for a moment, then returned to the car, drove to the rear of the service station, and again descended to the pavement. He removed his coat, reached into the glove compartment and produced a snub-nosed .32 revolver and shoulder holster, slipped it on, tested the breakaway several times, then loaded the revolver and snapped it into place. "Kwang Tri, my ass!" he muttered as he drew on the coat.

3

Twenty minutes later a hot little sports car eased through the arched gateway and along the parking ramp of a flashy apartment complex and came to rest in an open spot opposite the oval-shaped swimming pool. A tall man wearing dark glasses unwound from the small vehicle and stepped out onto the multicolored flagstones, coolly surveyed the swiming scene at poolside, then set off across the patio and through the near-nude swarm of life encamped there. Blazing lights provided glaring illumination in the darkness. Several hi-fis were going full blast in a cacaphony of mod sounds, but not even the electronic amplifications could overcome the noise level of scores of energetic voices raised in breathless chatter and excited revelry.

A large blonde in a minibikini was go-going from atop the shoulders of two bronzed youths out at pool center; a shriekingly amused girl was trying to hand a tall glass up to her. Bolan grinned to himself and shook his head against the frantic din, halting momentarily to consult a building directory at the base of the outside stairway. A dazzling beauty in a flesh-colored bikini came down the stairs, carefully balancing a tray of drinks. Bolan stood aside to let her pass; instead, she pushed the tray toward him. His right hand jerked instinctively towards the opening in his coat, then froze in relaxed constraint as the near nudie giggled and said, "Name your numbness, baby."

Bolan smiled. "I'm not in the party," he told her. "Thanks just the same."

"This's no party. This's a way of life." Her voice was slurred in alcoholic realization. "Get into something revealing and come on down." She giggled again and went on her way, hips swaying in the certain knowledge that her departure was being appreciatively watched.

Bolan went on up the stairs, paused at the first landing to gaze down on the swinging scene below, then continued slowly to the third level. Each apartment opened onto the courtyard; the level-three porch was deserted. Doors along Bolan's route of travel stood open, as though the entire building housed one big, swinging family. It seemed probable that most of the tenants were at poolside. The noise from below seemed to amplify as it rose toward the higher levels. Bolan wondered vaguely how anybody could live in such a racket.

He found the door he sought, conspicuously closed, and pressed the announcer. A peephole opened almost immediately, and an eye glared out at him. "Yeah?" a muffled voice said.

"George Zitka," the tall man replied. "He live here?"

"That's the name on the door, isn't it?"

"I don't believe everything I read." Bolan removed his sunglasses and dropped them into a coat pocket, the hand remaining to hover near the opening in the coat. "Is that you, Zitter?"

"Yeah." The peephole closed quickly, and the door cracked open. Bolan cast a quick glance right and left, then launched his 200-plus pounds into a vicious kick against the partially open door, following through with a rolling tumble into the darkened apartment.

Explosive reports and sizzling projectiles provided the welcome as several handguns unloaded in rapid fire, the muzzle flashes triangulating along his route of entry. Bolan's own weapon found his hand even as he was twisting across the floor, and a new sound was added to the gunfire symphony. A grunt and a thud near the open doorway announced the results of the first retort, and

5

already the second and third words were being introduced into the reply. Then there was silence, except for a sighing groan off to one corner of the room.

"Zitter?" Bolan called out softly.

"Zitter," came an immediate reply. "That you, Mack?"

"It's me." Bolan was rolling slowly as he spoke. "You okay, Zit?"

"Yeah. There's three of 'em. You get all three?"

"Check—three," Bolan replied. He sighed and got to his feet, returned to the door and found the light switch, then closed the door and turned on the lights.

Three men were lying about the small room like grotesque statues of death. Zitka sat in a corner on the floor, ropes binding his wrists and ankles. Bolan produced a pocket knife and cut the ropes. "You should have told your buddies the password," he said, grinning.

"Buddies hell!" Zitka muttered. "What'd you do to your hair?" He was rubbing the circulation into his hands and feet.

"Bleached it," Bolan said. "Cute huh? Tried the mustache route too but couldn't stand the filthy thing. What'd you let them tie you up for?"

Zitka growled an unintelligible response and reached for a pack of cigarettes on a nearby table. A dark man, heavily built, he moved with surprising grace. He was dressed only in a swimsuit.

Bolan had moved to one of the dead and was busily searching pockets and laying the contents out for inspection. "How'd you know they weren't cops?" he asked off-handedly.

"Cops don't slap you around and tie you up like a turkey," Zitka growled.

Bolan nodded. "They're Maffios," he reported. "Dammit, I *told* you to stay clear."

6

Bolan smiled and moved to the next body. "Thanks for the tip. But the ambush at Kwang Tri was a helluva lot hotter than *this* one."

"These bastards ain't playing games, Mack."

Bolan was still smiling. "Weren't much of a match for a couple of old jungle fighters, were they? Pretty cute the way you tipped me, Zit. Of all places to go for R and R. Kwang Tri, for God's sake."

"Yeah," Zitka said sourly. He had yet to find a glint of humor in the situation.

"How long they been encamped, Zit?"

"The big guy there has been hanging around a coupla days. I knew he was reconning. I figured they had a phone tap on me. The TV and papers here were full of your private little war with the Mafia. I had the setup figured, all right. The phone was tapped. Soon as you hung up they came busting in here. Hell, I hadn't been worried until I got your call, Mack. You're the last guy on earth I expected to show up here. You shoulda stayed clear. You really should've."

Bolan's smile became a dark scowl. "I couldn't stay clear, Zit," he replied. "The bastards have backtracked my entire life. I found stakeouts every place I went. They were waiting for me in Omaha, in Denver, at Gordon's place up in Evergreen, at Vegas—and now here. It's getting to be too damn much, Zit, Dammit, I need . . ." His voice trailed off, and he raised baffled eyes to his friend.

"What you need, buddy, is a miracle," Zitka declared. His eyes dropped. "And what I need is to get this garbage the hell out of here."

Bolan sighed. "Call the cops, Zit. Tell them what happened. Meanwhile I'll be fading across the nearest horizon."

"You want me to kick the hell right outta you?" Zitka fumed.

7

"This isn't your war," Bolan said quietly. "No need for you to get involved."

"Shut up, just shut up!" Zitka said angrily. "I wouldn't even *be* here if you hadn't dragged my riddled ass out of Phung Duc."

"I just don't want—"

"*Screw* what you don't want. You came here, didn't you? Awright, you're here, and I ain't blowing no whistles! Let's just get these stiffs to hell out of my apartment. Then we'll figure out what to do next. But you ain't fading across no horizons, buddy." He held out his hand, and Bolan gripped it tightly. "Now unless I'm up there scoutin' for you."

They shook hands solemnly, then stood quietly surveying the latest carnage of The Executioner's war. Bolan kicked lightly at a dead foot. "Don't suppose anybody's tumbled to the gunfire yet," he murmured. "Not with all the other racket around here. What kind of joint is this, Zit? Does this noise go on all the time?"

"Just about." Zitka smiled. "Places like this are the new scene, Mack. Residence club, it's called— for swinging singles only. I had to lie about my age to get this apartment. Would you believe I'm in the older generation?"

Bolan chuckled. "The guys over in 'Nam don't really know what they're fighting for, do they? Well . . . I'm driving a 'Vette. It makes a lousy garbage truck. What kind of car do you have?"

"It'll serve as a garbage scow," Zitka replied. "The only way outta here, though, is out through the patio. We'll have to lug them right through the swingers."

"From what I saw, it wouldn't be too startling a sight," Bolan said musingly. "Well, let's give it a try. You lead the way."

Zitka picked up a keycase from a corner table,

then carefully positioned a body on the floor and heaved it onto his shoulder. Bolan swung on aboard in a fireman's carry and followed Zitka onto the porch and down the stairway. He found it weirdly incredible that such a short time had elapsed since he had climbed those stairs. The revelries at poolside seemed unchanged, except that now the blonde go-going in the pool had been joined by several others; they seemed to have some sort of contest going. Someone shouted a greeting to Zitka, and a playful couple nearly spilled Bolan and his corpse into the pool. Otherwise, they were totally ignored. Bolan paused alongside a table to reposition his load. He smiled at a gargantuan-chested cutie in a technically topless swimsuit, lifted her glass to his lips and tasted it, then thanked her and went on. He found Zitka stuffing a body into the rear seat of a late-model Dodge and added his own burden to the repository.

Zitka was huffing with exertion and complaining about his feet and the rough pavement. "One to go," Bolan declared. He was pushing at a protruding foot and trying to close the car door.

"Let me get him," Zitka said. "I need to get into some clothes anyway. I'll make it fast." He hurried back toward the patio. Bolan walked over to his Corvette, took a handful of ammo from the glove compartment, and dropped it into his coat pocket. Then he returned to the Dodge, reloaded his weapon, lit a cigarette, and waited. The cigarette was less than half-gone when Zitka reappeared, dressed in jeans, a knit shirt, and deck shoes and carrying the third gunman.

A car swept up the drive at that precise instant, catching Zitka in the full glare of the headlights. It halted with a lurching bounce, as though the driver had floorboarded the brake pedal; doors on each side were flung open, and a flurry of human activity erupted around the vehicle. Jungle instincts moved Bolan into a flying dive across the Dodge just as the chatter of an automatic weapon laced the night air above the sounds of patio revelry. Projectiles were zipping into the Dodge in a full sweep from bumper to bumper. In the periphery of his vision, Bolan noted that the dead gunman who had been on Zitka's shoulder was now lying across the trunk of a parked automobile; Zitka himself was not in sight. Bolan's .32 was in his hand, but it seemed small comfort in the face of the burpgun that was methodically spraying the area about him. He rolled and crawled along the line of parked cars until he was directly opposite the attacking vehicle.

Another chattergun had joined the action, one on either side of the car now, and the fire was still being directed in the general direction of the Dodge. A pistol cracked from somewhere downrange, then again; both headlamps of the enemy car shattered, and the lights went out. One of the gunmen yelled a muffled warning, and one of the automatics began spraying the car upon which Zitka had dumped the body.

Bolan smiled grimly; Zit was in the action—he had anticipated Bolan's movement and was providing diversionary fire. The gas tank of the latest target exploded in a spectacular fireball. An unfamiliar voice cried, "Goddammit! Lookit that!" Bolan jerked to his feet just as a nattily dressed man pounded around the line of cars; his .32 arced up and exploded, and the man hit the pavement and slid grotesquely into a fetal ball.

One does not plan each successive step of a firefight. Actions in warfare proceed from the instincts, not from the intellect, and Bolan's first shot, at such proximity to the enemy, of necessity became a fusillade. Diving and shooting, rolling and shooting, eyes ever on the enemy—these are the dictates of effective warfare at eyeball range, and The Executioner knew them well. One chatter-gun was silenced by his third shot. The other gun-man had spun to the rear of the vehicle and was frantically trying to bring the spraying track onto Bolan's furious advance. There was not time. Bolan's fifth shot tore into the gun arm; the sixth impacted squarely on the bridge of the nose even before the heavy weapon could fall to the ground, and man and chatterer went to earth together.

Another man scampered around the front fender of the vehicle, firing wildly with a pistol, the bullets singing past Bolan and ricocheting into automobiles behind him. Bolan's .32 was empty. He went into motion, leaping toward cover, just as Zitka stepped into the open, pistol raised to shoulder level, and popped two shots into the other man's chest. Silence descended. Even the patio was quiet. The burning automobile was lending an eerie quality to the silence. A gradually growing babble of excitement was beginning to issue from the patio area.

Zitka had run over to the Dodge and was dragging the dead bodies out onto the pavement. Bolan moved swiftly to the Corvette, started it, and swung toward the Dodge, slowing down for Zitka to jump in, then gunned down the ramp and onto the street. Zitka relaxed into the backrest. "Got that garbage to hell out of my car," he panted.

"Let the cops figure it," Bolan clipped. He was heading west; moments later they intersected the coast highway and swung southward.

"Wonder if the insurance company will pay off," Zitka worried aloud.

"Huh?" Bolan was driving leisurely now, allowing his nervous system to get its pace.

11

"My car. Did you see it? Full of holes. Tore all to hell. I bet the bastards won't pay off."

"Welcome back to the war," Bolan said.

"I didn't know I'd miss it so much."

"You serious?"

"Sure I'm serious. Haven't had so much fun since I got back to this vale of tears."

They drove in silence for several minutes. Zitka lit a cigarette, handed it to Bolan, then lit another for himself. Presently, Bolan said, "You're a good friend, Zit."

"I better be."

"Huh?"

"I said, I better be. There's a hundred grand on your head, Mack. Big guy back there offered to cut me in."

"Yeah?"

A momentary silence; then: "Yeah. A hundred grand. They sure must love you."

"You wouldn't finger me for the Mafia, Zit," Bolan observed quietly. "Not for money. For fun, maybe, yeah—but not for money."

"It'd be a hell of a game, wouldn't it?" Zitka mused.

"What would?"

"If I decided to try collecting that hundred grand. I wonder which one of us would wind up dead."

"You would," Bolan replied unemotionally.

"Think so?"

"Yeah. I wouldn't want to kill you, Zit. But I would. If I had to."

"I guess you would. It'd still be a hell of a game."

"I guess so."

Zitka chuckled merrily. "A real grand slammer. Don't take me serious, Mack."

"If you're looking for some fun—the odds are a

12

lot farther out on my side. Don't even count the cops. They're gentlemen. Just count the junkies, the punks, hoods, goons, and gunsels, the amateurs and the pro's and just any guy with a sudden hungering for a large chunk of greens. Back them up with the Mafia, the best-organized crime syndicate in the world, and every contractor in the business. There's odds, Zit. If it's fun you want . . ."

"I said don't take me serious," Zitka protested. "Hell, I had my chance to throw in with them, and I turned 'em down flat."

"We work good together, Zit."

Zitka sighed. "Let's go somewhere and get a drink."

"Sorry. Bars are off-limits to me now, Zit. One little rhubarb and I'm behind bars. How about some coffee?"

"Naw. Let's just drive and talk. I think we got something to talk out."

"Okay."

"What's your plans?"

"I thought I'd look up Jim Brantzen."

"*Doc* Brantzen?"

"Yeah. He's out now and in civilian practice. Cosmetic surgery, he calls it. Remember that raid at Dak To? He's always figured he owes me something for that. I figure maybe I'll see if he still feels that way."

"Gonna get your face changed, eh?"

Bolan grinned. "I hate to part with it, but I guess it's the only thing to do. I can't go on jumping at every shadow that rears up in my path."

"So you're running from the Mafia?"

"I didn't say that. I just need a camouflage job, that's all. I'm not calling off the war."

13

Zitka sighed again. "In that case, then—are enlistments open?"

Bolan threw him a fast scrutiny. "You want to join up?"

"I guess I already have."

"Yeah. I guess you have. You'll be on their list now for sure. For damn sure."

"I been thinking, too," Zitka announced.

"About what?"

"You figure the Mafia is in a fat-cat position around here?"

"I figure that."

"You figure I could be of any use to you?"

Bolan snickered. "Whispering Death Zitka? Hey, buddy, I've been there, remember? Quang So, Hwa Tring, Chak Dong—yeah, I figure you could be of some use."

"You need some reinforcements, Mack."

"Yeah, I'll buy that."

"Well, I been thinking. Lot of guys come back from Vietnam and find it hard blending back into the tedium of civilian life. Like me. And like Boom-Boom Hoffower."

Bolan raised his eyebrows and flashed a sidewise glance at his companion. "You've been in touch with Boom-Boom?"

"Yeah, he has a pad out in Laurel Canyon, dying of boredom. His wife run off with some actor, and he didn't even get excited about that. Best damn demolition man this side of the China Sea, Mack—just sitting around bored to death."

"Are you saying I could get some troops like Boom-Boom to join my war?" Bolan asked quietly.

"If you made it interesting enough."

"Mercenaries," Bolan said.

"Sure. Why not? You're fighting a bunch of mercenaries, aren't you? Fight fire with fire. I imagine you could figure some way to make this war profitable. How much did you pay for this little bomb?"

"It can be profitable," Bolan assured him. "The Mafia transacts a lot of cash business. There's always a pile of green wherever they may be. I've had my hands in it."

"Well, there you are," Zitka said, sighing. "Me, I'd do it just for the hell of it. But like any game, it's more interesting with some cash on the table. And think of what a troop of jungle professionals could add to your odds, Mack. I bet we could get—"

"Okay, I'm thinking about it," Bolan snapped. "Be quiet now and let me think."

"So think," Zitka growled.

Bolan smiled and drove on in silence. They passed through Manhattan Beach and continued on at a leisurely pace. Zitka sighed several times and drummed his fingers on the seat. Bolan was coming to a fateful decision. Presently he lit a cigarette, slowly exhaled the smoke, and said, "Okay."

"Okay what?" Zitka sniffed.

"Ten of us. That's all. Tight, effective, mobile— and every man a specialist. At least two more sharpshooters. Two scouts, as good as you. Boom-Boom or an equal. Two heavy-weapons men. A good technician. That's it."

"Ten isn't very many," Zitka complained.

"It's enough. I don't want a damn army. A squad. A death squad, that's it. It gets too big, it gets unmanageable. I rule. I say shit, they squat and ask what color. I say when to hit, what to hit, how to hit."

"Has to be that way."

Bolan nodded his head soberly. "First man steps out of line or turns renegade gets shot on the spot. They'll have to understand that. We live under combat rules at all times."

"It'll work," Zitka said. "They'll accept that."

"They'll have to, or it's no game, Zit. And they'll have to understand they'll be playing long odds— mighty long odds. It will be a death game, Zit."

"That's the only kind would be worthwhile for the kind of guys I'm thinking of." He showed Bolan a faint smile. "I been playing the death game most of my adult life. Haven't you?"

Bolan nodded curtly. "The name of the game will be Hit the Mafia. We'll hit them so fast, so often, and from so many directions they'll think hell fell in on them. We steal 'em blind, see. We kill and we terrorize and we take every goddamned thing they have—and then we'll see how powerful and well organized they are."

Zitka shot his friend an appraising stare. A nerve ticked in his cheek, and a small thrill chased down his spine. It seemed ridiculous, but he felt a flicker of pity for the Mafia. He had worked with The Executioner before, many times, in the jungles of Vietnam. Now the jungles were moving to Mafialand.

"Well, what do you say?" Bolan asked tersely.

"I say, on to the games, James," Zitka replied quietly. "Turn this bomb around. I'll show you how to get to Laurel Canyon."

Bolan swung into a roadside park and back onto the highway, reversing his direction. His foot grew heavy on the accelerator. "The game is on," he murmured.

Chapter Two

THE DEATH SQUAD

Bill (Boom-Boom) Hoffower, the demolitions expert, was pulled away from a five-day drunk, sobered up, and recruited with a two-minute pitch. The twenty-six-year-old ex-Quaker from Pennsylvania, a blond and blue-eyed six footer, found the proposition immediately intriguing. He had only slightly known Bolan in Vietnam and had heard nothing whatever of The Executioner's recent exploits in the East. The Mafia he had always regarded as an American fantasy ("You telling me there really is a Mafia?"). His decision to join the death squad had nothing to do with friendship or idealism. Until recently he had been employed by an oil company in offshore drilling operations. He had deserted the job shortly after his wife deserted him and had not worked "for a couple of months."

Hoffower demonstrated to Bolan his expertise with explosives by "disarming" his own home. "The mortgage people are coming out Tuesday to take it back," he confided. "I got it rigged to blow it up in their goddamn faces."

Bolan was impressed with Hoffower's knowhow and was, of course, cognizant of the demolition expert's Vietnam reputation. Not only did he possess a golden touch with explosives, but he had also proved himself as a coolly capable combat infantryman. Hoffower was left sober, a thousand dollars wealthier, and with "forty-hours, delay in reporting" to settle his personal affairs.

Tom (Bloodbrother) Loudelk was recruited by telephone from the Blackfoot Reservation in Montana. He had worked with both Bolan and Zitka in

17

various military operations, and he agreed to the proposition with only the sketchiest of information, even before he was told of the thousand-dollar "enlistment bonus." He promised to be in Los Angeles "as soon as I can sell three cows and clean the manure outta my fingernails."

Loudelk had been released to the dubious joys of the reservation only two months earlier. He had been the most fantastically effective advance scout in Bolan's memory, surpassing even Zitka in nerveless efficiency. In Vietnam Loudelk had personally accounted for sixty-seven enemy dead, yet had fired not a single shot. He was an expert with a knife and had developed to a fine art the technique of snapping a human neck with one swift movement of bare hands.

They found Angelo (Chopper) Fontenelli in a topless pizza parlor and bar in Santa Monica, where he had been employed as a combination doorman, bouncer, and maitre d'. The twenty-four-year-old native of New Jersey, though only slightly more than five and a half feet tall, was not often a party to casual disputes. Powerfully built from the ground up, with mammoth chest and shoulders, thick and squat, the tough little Italian ranked high in Bolan's respect.

Chopper was so called because of his expertise with heavy automatic weapons. One year earlier he had covered the withdrawal after one of Bolan's sniping missions, single handedly plugging a battalion-strength pursuit by the enemy for nearly an hour before being reinforced by helicopter gunships. He listened attentively to the recruiting pitch, wet his lips nervously each time the word "Mafia" was spoken, then accepted the stack of crisp twenties from Bolan with the simple comment: "Jesus—never thought it could happen, but I'm so sick o' titties I could puke."

Fontenelli came into the Death Squad complete with his own weaponry: a fifty-caliber water-cooled machine gun; one of the new gatling-type superguns salvaged from a crashed Magic Dragon gunship; and a complete arsenal of miscellaneous light automatics representing the best from both sides of the Vietnam conflict. How he had acquired this private collection and transported it to the United States was Fontenelli's own secret; he pointedly avoided any discussion of the subject but gladly "rented" his arsenal to the Death Squad.

Juan (Flower Child) Andromede was rehabilitated from a reality cult in the North Hollywood hills where he had become known as "Fra Juanito" eleven short months after his recognition as "the Butcher of Tanh Vin." Also a heavy-weapons man, Andromede was a poetry-spouting mass-death expert who used a field mortar like a six-gun. He was also highly proficient with various other types of light artillery and had been widely respected in the delta for his uncanny ability to operate independently of spotters and other fire-control techniques. An unusual product of New York's ghettos, the mild-mannered Puerto Rican signaled his acceptance of Bolan's recruiting efforts with the quiet statement: "Only the dead can accept heaven. Hell is for the living. A thousand bills advance money, eh? Okay. I accept hell."

Andromede was twenty-three, lightly built, deceptively delicate appearing. He brought out the mother instinct in women and inspired middle-aged men to call him "son." He verbally deplored violence, wore peace beads day and night, and stoutly denied that he had ever killed. "I didn't kill those people I liberated them. Death is the liberation of the entity." In Vietnam, he had "liberated" several hundred entities.

Herman (Gadgets) Schwarz was plucked from a technical school on the east side of Los Angeles, where he had been taking a course designed to equip him with an FCC license in radio electronics. Schwarz was one of those rare individuals who know more instinctively than their instructors know deliberately. He strongly resented living in a world that was more impressed by academic exercises than by demonstrated ability. "No license, no job," had been the message from his society, so Schwarz had reluctantly submitted to the indignities of classroom formality. After five months of "esoteric nonsense," the electronics genius was altogether ready for Bolan's proposition. He had been a counterintelligence advisor in Vietnam and had once "bugged" a VC command bunker to gain intelligence from a Bolan-Zitka sniper-team operation. Bolan had been deeply impressed by Schwarz's cool and painstaking methodology and was particularly elated to number him in the Death Squad. Once, according to official record, Schwarz had lain for six days in high grass at the edge of a VC stronghold, gathering intelligence with a directional microphone and a pocket recorder. Bolan regarded him as a formidable weapon in his war against the Mafia.

Jim (Gunsmoke) Harrington was flushed from a suburban Los Angeles amusement park, where he was employed as a "gunfighter." One of the few men to Bolan's knowledge who had been allowed to carry personal weapons into battle, Harrington had brought the image of the old West into the firefights of Vietnam, with two six-guns worn in quick-draw fashion. It had not been all image—his Colts were equipped with specially designed hair triggers. This youngster from an Idaho sheep ranch could draw both guns and hit a fast-moving target at a hundred feet more quickly than most men could think about it. He had been Bolan's flank man on a score of sniping missions and had repeatedly demonstrated his value in the sudden eyeball encounters with the enemy that were so common on the deep-penetration strikes. With .44-caliber ammunition worse than scarce in the combat theater, Bolan had endeared himself to Harrington by helping him set up a makeshift armory in which he could make his own ammo.

Harrington was also a deadly sharpshooter with a rifle, preferring the light semiautomatic carbine, and had proved especially effective in a quick-firing, running fight.

For fourteen months he had staged sixteen "gunfights" daily, six days per week, at the amusement park. He had been fully and anxiously aware of the executioner's trouble at Pittsfield. Bolan had no opportunity whatever to deliver his offer of "employment." Harrington recognized him immediately, even through the camouflage of bleached hair and dark glasses. "Thank God," the twenty-two-year-old ex-sheepherder declared happily. "I thought you'd never get here. You need my gun, don't you? Thank God. Come on, let's get outta this frigged-up funnyland. I been firing blanks for fourteen months. Thank God—thank God you're here!"

Mark (Deadeye) Washington certainly had no integrated blood in his veins, unless it was a fusion of the darkest African tribes. He was the blackest black man Bolan had ever known—and certainly the most dangerous. Washington's specialty was the big high-powered distance rifle with the twenty-power sniperscope. Like Bolan, he had been a sniper specialist. Bolan had only once witnessed Washington's craft—Mark had dropped three running targets from five hundred yards out, and the feat ruled out any possibility of luck or chance. Bolan knew that one does not luck onto three scurrying men a third of a mile away; once was enough to assure Deadeye Washington a chunk of Bolan's respect.

The big Negro came from a unpainted three-room shack on Mississippi's Gulf Coast—and it had not been necessary to draft Mark Washington from the environment. He had joined the army on his eighteenth birthday, several weeks before his scheduled graduation from the dismal little Negro high school, and he had never gone back—not even to pick up his diploma. He had voluntarily extended his duty tour twice, for a total of thirty-three months of combat duty. Then he'd decided to come home and find out what the Black Power business was all about. Less than five weeks later, The Executioner traced him to a one-room echo of Mississippi in a place called Watts. Bolan quietly stated his proposition, and again no draft was necessary. Mark Washington had always known what "black power" was. It was the same as any other kind of human power. It was, simply, manhood. Manhood's highest expression, for Mark Washington, had been found with a big gun and a twenty-power scope.

Rosario Blancanales had started his Vietnam adventure as a member of the special forces. He had understood the Vietnamese, perhaps simply because he'd wanted to understand them, and he had learned their language and their ways. He had proved himself highly effective in the pacification program, was known throughout the delta as, simply, Politician, and had been an invaluable guide on several of Bolan's penetration missions. He was a pretty fair medic and a gifted mechanic, and he could hold his own in a firefight.

Bolan wanted Blancanales primarily because of the man's chameleonlike ability to blend into any environment. He respected the thirty-four-year-old's natural gift for organization and administration, and he had imagined that some day the Blancanales charm would find an outlet in U.S. politics. He found him, instead, working as an orderly in a veterans' hospital.

"You caught me just in time," Blancanales told Bolan. "I was going down tomorrow to reenlist." The Politician had found an environment he could not blend into. He leaped at Bolan's offer of a new one.

Blancanales took over the remains of Bolan's "purse," some several thousand dollars remaining from the spoils of the Pittsfield battle, and attended to the immediate problems of logistics support. He rented a large and comfortable beach house in a lonely area north of Santa Monica and stocked it with foodstuffs and other necessities. The "first formation" of the Death Squad was accomplished on the afternoon of September 24, with all members reporting into the beachside "base camp." Blancanales had already seen to billeting assignments. Schwarz immediately set about developing an electronic-security system. Hoffower undertook a terrain inspection, with an eye to the emplacement of personnel mines and other defensive devices. Zitka and Loudelk began a thorough recon of the entire area, toward the establishment of forward defense positions. Harrington and Andromede began work on the armory. Fontenelli and Washington repaired to the beach to set up a target range in the shadow of the cliffs. Bolan and Blancanales went to San Bernardino to ferret out a contact for the procurement of arms and munitions.

Chapter Three

THE SOFT PROBE

In the early morning hours of September 27, a trunk line carrying telephone service to an exclusive Bel Air neighborhood was severed. A resident of the area pinpointed the time of the interruption at precisely 6:10 A.M.; she had been conversing with an airline ticket agent at the airport in Inglewood when the connection was lost.

An elderly man who lives in the gardener's cottage at the rear of the Giordano estate in Bel Air also pinpointed 6:10 A.M. as the moment when an uninvited guest walked through his back door, interrupting him at breakfast. The visitor was a wiry, dark-skinned man who "walked like a cat." He wore faded blue jeans, a denim jacket, Indian mocassins, and a rag tied about his forehead. A military web belt with ammunition pouches supported a .45-caliber automatic in a flap-type holster. A long dagger was on the other hip. The interloper bound the gardener with a nylon rope and taped a clean gauze bandage across his mouth, then carried him to the bedroom and gently placed him on the bed.

Moments after the man departed, the gardener, looking through his bedroom window, saw a man in a "black, tight-fitting outfit" drop over the wall surrounding the estate and move quickly toward the main house. Another man immediately followed, this one carrying a heavy weapon slung about his shoulders.

At about that same time, a chauffeur on the bordering estate to the north looked out the window of his garage apartment, to see a man in army fatigues—"and wearing six-guns, I swear"—sprinting across the property toward the Giordano estate. The chauffeur tried to call the police, but his telephone was dead.

Also at about 6:10, an early-rising housekeeper was walking a pet along the curving lane fronting the property. She was startled by the sudden appearance of a military jeep "with two soldiers in it and a big gun in the back." The vehicle halted at the driveway to the Giordano estate, then backed across the sidewalk with the heavy machine gun commanding the front of the house. The woman fled, after being advised by one of the men to "walk your dog in some other part of hell, lady."

At 6:13 A.M. the sedate neighborhood was jarred by a muffled explosion and a volley of gunshots. A small group of household employees staggered down the front walk at Giordano's an instant later, led by a man in army fatigues. Some were still clad in nightclothes. They were ushered to the street and withdrew to the other side, clustering together in a hushed knot. Their guide hurried down to the jeep, spoke briefly to the driver, then ran back toward the house. Moments later the jeep bounced onto the street and careered about for a U-turn into the Giordano driveway, accelerating along the curving drive toward the house and trailing a dense black smokescreen, then emerged at the other side and sped up the street with the smoke pot at full delivery.

The entire area was now blanketed in a dense pall of smoke, but witnesses could still hear sporadic gunfire from within the mansion and the occasional rattling burp of an automatic weapon.

Silence descended at precisely 6:16 A.M., the time verified by various witnesses. The old man in the gardener's cottage viewed apprehensively the reappearance of the man in the faded jeans. The man slashed the gardener's bonds, patted him on the head, and walked calmly out the door.

The first police cruiser to reach the scene did not arrive until 6:22, just moments ahead of the fire trucks and with the smokescreen beginning to dissipate. Spectators clustered about the police car to deliver breathless reports of the incident. The patrolman immediately radioed for reinforcements and restrained the fire department from entering the premises. Two additional cruisers arrived within minutes. The police then made a careful advance onto the property. A bullet-riddled, pajama-clad corpse was found in the lower hallway, just inside the house, an unfired pistol beneath the crumpled body. The dining room of the mansion had obviously been raked by machine-gun fire; furnishings were splintered; all four walls exhibited multiple punctures at chest-level; china and other fragile items were shattered.

The body of another man, this one fully clothed and wearing gun leather, was found in an upstairs sitting room. His skull was a bloodied pulp, smashed by the impact of numerous steel-jacketed slugs. One wall of an adjoining bedroom had been destroyed by an explosive blast, the gaping remains of a wall safe bearing mute testimony as to cause and effect.

At 6:30 the police found Emilio Giordano, owner of the property. Jack Matsumura, the gardener, was holding a lonely vigil and sadly contemplating his employer's state of being from a respectful distance. Giordano was apparently alive and unharmed but, in Patrolman Harold Kalb's assessment of the situation, "in one hell of a fix." The millionaire was spread-eagled across a fertilizer pile at the edge of a flower garden, face-down, wrists and ankles tied to wooden stakes. Giordano was completely naked, and he was booby trapped.

26

A bewildering maze of fine wires criss-crossed over and under his body, terminating in a taut arrangement with the pins of two hand grenades, one between his hands and the other between his knees. A large black hand had been painted onto the flesh of his back.

Kalb sent another patrolman to radio for the bomb detail, then knelt gingerly close by and tried to comfort and reassure the carefully breathing victim. Giordano would risk not even the muscular contractions of speech, and it was a strange and strained twenty-minute wait for the experts of the demolitions squad.

Following another few minutes of painstaking and nerveracking work by the bomb unit, it was discovered that the grenades were nothing but practice dummies. Giordano became hysterically enraged and fainted. It was sometime past eight o'clock before the police were able to question the fifty-year-old millionnaire, and even then he could add very little to their meager knowledge of the circumstances surrounding the crime.

According to Giordano, he was awakened by a tall man with blond hair who was weirdly suited "in an outfit like the commandos used to wear." The man was pressing the muzzle of a military-style .45 automatic against the base of Giordano's nose. The man ordered him to get out of bed. Giordano habitually slept nude; he tried to get dressed, but the man shoved him into the hallway before he could make a move toward his clothing.

Another man hurried out of the room behind them; the blast came an instant later. The tall man escorted Giordano down the stairs. "And by some other nuts who were shooting up the place" and into the rear yard. Another man (". . . looked like an Indian") joined them there. "They threw me on that pile of filth," Giordano related, "and told me

I could live for as long as I could lie perfectly still. How was I to know those things weren't real?"

Giordano identified the two dead men as his security guards but professed total ignorance of the identity of the intruders. The significance of the black hand that had been painted upon his back was not lost on the detective sergeant who questioned him; Giordano himself, however, offered no reason whatever why his tormentors would have done such a thing. He cited robbery as the only possible motive for the attack but declined even to estimate the amount of cash stolen.

A general shakedown of the area by the police yielded few additional clues. A uniformed security guard two blocks away from the scene reported the passing of a military vehicle carrying two men and a heavy gun "a few minutes after the explosion." Two attendants of a service station at the major intersection just beyond that point, however, were certain that no such vehicle had come their way. They had heard the explosion also and had been looking for some sign of unusual activity. They were unable to report the disturbance, they added, because their telephone had gone dead minutes earlier.

The police investigation continued in the Bel Air neighborhood through out most of the morning. At ten o'clock a hurriedly requested police file was being verifaxed from Pittsfield to Los Angeles. At 11:30 a hastily convened police conference at the Los Angeles Hall of Justice was told, "It would appear that Mack Bolan, the man called The Executioner, has come to Los Angeles. Apparently, he has not come alone. It would seem that he has brought a private army with him. All hell is going to break loose in this city unless we can do our job quickly and effectively. This is to be a maximum effort. *Get Bolan!*"

As these words were being spoken, the object of police concern was conducting a conference of his own. The scene was a comfortable beach house a few miles north of Santa Monica. The Terrible Ten were assembled on the patio. The atmosphere was informal and relaxed. Bundles of currency were stacked on a glass-topped table. The tinkling of ice against glass was the only sound as Mack Bolan lit a cigarette. He rocked his chair back to balance on the rear legs and quietly announced, "Well, it was a bit sloppy here and there, but we'll get better. We'll have to. In a soft probe like this one, timing isn't all that important, but . . ." He pinned Blancanales with a hard stare. "Politician, you were forty seconds early with that smokescreen. Bloodbrother was still wiring the grenades when the smoke got to us. If those had been live grenades . . ."

"I got worried," Blancanales admitted. "Too many spectators. I was afraid somebody would do something stupid."

Bolan nodded his acceptance of the deviation and turned his gaze onto Fontenelli. "Good show with the jeep, Chopper. Beautifully executed. I guess the cops are still searching Bel Air for it."

Fontenelli grinned, warming noticeably under the praise. "I hope it drives 'em nuts," he said.

"How much goop did you use, Boom?" Bolan asked musingly, shifting to Hoffower.

"You said enough to eject the safe. I ejected it."

Bolan grinned. "You sure did. To the other side of the room. I was wondering if we could have gotten along with a bit less goop, though. That blast must have been heard clear down at city hall."

"Yeah, I overdid it a little," Hoffower said lightly. "First time I ever blew a safe. I added a bit of fudge factor, just in case."

Bolan blew a cloud of cigarette smoke at the

stacks of currency, then picked up a packet and tossed it at Hoffower. "This is the way it looks after a good blow," he said. "Now picture a pile of green confetti, and that's how it would look after a bad blow. Keep that in mind."

Hoffower grinned and tossed the money onto the table. "I'll keep 'em good."

Zitka coughed, cleared his throat, then said, "Okay, tell me how late I was gettin' the civilians out."

"Almost a full minute," Bolan replied evenly. "The old colored man downstairs was caught in Gunsmoke's crossfire. If Gunsmoke hadn't shoved him into the pantry . . . well . . . What delayed you, Zitter?"

"The upstairs maid was on the can," Zitka solemnly reported. "I hurried her all I could."

An amused titter ran through the squad. Someone said, "Praise the Lord and pass the toilet paper." Zitka turned flaming red.

"So we learned a lesson," Bolan commented, when the laughter had subsided. "We need to plan the human element into future timetables. Let's keep it in mind."

"You just can't figure everything," Zitka groused.

"So—that puts the burden of individual initiation on everyone's shoulders," Bolan replied. He angled his gaze toward Schwarz. "You have any problems, Gadgets?" he asked quietly.

Schwarz soberly shook his head. "Timing was great from my standpoint. I was up out of that PT and T manhole at 6:05, on the button." He winked at Hoffower. "Only way to cut a cable, man. Get with me someday, Boom, and show me how to make those little specialties. Anyway, the timer was set for 6:10. I left Flower there, at the manhole, and cut across to the house. Got there at 6:12. Went in right behind the blast. Planted my

30

little gems and was clear at 6:15. Picked up Flower Child at 6:19, and here we are."

"No trouble at the cable," Andromede reported. "Went off at 6:10, right on schedule. Sizzle, crack, pop—that easy. But oh, my nerves!"

Mark Washington laughed softly. "I could see you poppin' up outta that hole," he told Andromede.

"Yeah?"

"Yeah. Had you right in my crosshairs. Scares bird turds outta you, handling those little explosives, don't it? If you'd been black like me, you'd have turned white."

"You could see me that good?" Andromede asked incredulously.

"Sure. When ol' twenty power lays onto you, the veins in your eyeballs looks like the Martian canals."

"How was your view of the house?" Bolan asked.

"Pretty fair, on the north side and the back. Too many trees in front, but I could get the general drift of things even there. At the rear, though, I could've picked off anybody trying to break out. I guess." Washington smiled and added, "Some lady was swimmin' naked down on the east slope."

"Yeah?" Harrington asked interestedly.

Washington was still smiling. "Yeah. 'bout two streets down, little round swimmin' pool in the backyard."

"How does a big, fat tit look in a twenty power?" Zitka asked.

"Like a big, fat tit, I guess," Washington replied evenly. "But this one's wasn't fat. They was skinny and pointy-lookin'."

"I saw you, Deadeye," Loudelk reported quietly, his voice rising softly above the ensuing chuckles.

Washington turned an owlish stare onto the Indian. "Huh?"

31

"I caught a couple of flashes from your scope," Loudelk explained. "You better remember that. When you're sighting toward the rising or setting sun, you better do something about reflections off your lens."

"I'll use the Polaroids next time," Washington mumbled humbly. "Thanks."

Bolan fidgeted slightly and asked, "Could you have covered our withdrawal okay, Deadeye? I mean, if there'd been a pursuit?"

"Some of you, sure. Not the jeep. Like I said, too many trees on that side. I could only catch a glimpse of things, now and then. You know how the twenty power reduces the field. But I did see the cops coming. I could have diverted them long before they ever got there—if I'd had to. Didn't have to, though. You had a three-minute lead on them. Now if some of those other cats had come poppin' outta the back of the house . . . well, the range was only just over 400 meters. Yeah. I could've covered that angle okay." He chuckled merrily. "And I could've plowed a furrow right up fat-ass's behind, the way you had him strung out there. Man, he wasn't even *breathin'* hard."

Bolan grinned. "It was good for his soul, I'm sure," he commented.

"Yeah." Washington tugged at the tip of his nose. "I'd like to tell you something, Sarge."

"Okay."

"You run a sweet hit. It looked good, mighty good, from where I was. I didn't see nothin' wrong with the timing. It went just like you said—even to the cops."

Bolan sobered. "It has to stay that way. And especially where the police are concerned. We have to avoid them at any cost."

"*Any* cost?" Fontenelli growled.

"That's what I said."

"I don't get this love affair with the fuzz," Fontenelli grumbled.

"You want to get yourself a bluesuiter, Chopper?" Bolan asked quietly.

"Not 'specially. But if it comes down to, like between me'n them—well . . ." Fontenelli cast a quick survey of the assembled faces. "Well . . . I'm not sure I'll want to break and run."

"You'd better break and run," Bolan said ominously. "You understand this. You deliberately shoot a cop, and you're out on your ass. Now understand it. You're out. I don't even like the contingency plan we had with Deadeye on today's strike. Shooting *at* a cop isn't much different than shooting *into* a cop, from the cop's point of view. All of you, now, understand this thoroughly. As long as we are just cleaning out the sewers, people will be rooting for us. Secretly, maybe, but still cheering. But you kill one cop, or one kid, or any other innocent bystander, and the cheering ends, soldier—it ends right there. The cops stop looking the other way and the news people stop romanticizing, and suddenly you're just another piece of sewer filth yourself. And then, Robin Hood, you're to hell out of business."

"Sure, sure," Fontenelli agreed quietly.

"All right." Bolan was studying the tips of his fingers. "I don't want to belabor the thing, but what I said in the beginning is just as certain as the sunrise. I'll shoot dead in his tracks any man who tries to turn this squad into a ratpack. There's still time to get out if anybody has decided he doesn't like the setup."

A strained, almost embarrassed silence ensued. Bolan gave it full play before he smiled, cleared his throat, and began speaking again. "Fine. We all know the score. Now let's talk about operations. Today's soft probe was a success from every angle.

33

Giordano was my only sure link with the western branch of the family. Now he knows we're in town. He knows we're onto him. We killed two of his boys, we wrecked his house, we took a chunk of money away from him, we humiliated him, and we showed him that he is living strictly at our pleasure." The smile broadened. "That's a helluva bitter mouthful for a Mafia honcho to chew on. He will be laying quiet for a few hours, at least until the cops stop poking around the neighborhood. Then he'll start braying like the tin god he is. He will start threshing around and flexing his muscles and demanding our heads on a Mafia platter. This is precisely what we want him to do."

Bolan turned an amused gaze onto his friend Zitka. "Remember that operation at Vanh Duc, Zitter?" he asked.

Zitka responded with a broad grin. "Yeah," he said, his gaze sweeping the circle of faces. "The Ninth was conducting a sweep into long-time VC territory. No contact, no contact, everywhere they probed. Knew damn well the northmen were around there, but they just kept fading away. All the Ninth flushed during a ten-day sweep was a bunch of terrorized villagers. So they sent us in."

His gaze flicked to Bolan and lingered there for a moment; then he chuckled and resumed the account. "It was Mack and me, two flankmen, two scouts. We walked for three days, and we knew where we was headed. We played the VC game, see. Hit and fade, hit and fade. By the time we'd penetrated to Vanh Duc, the VCs were screaming bloody murder. We'd already executed one of their generals, a half a dozen high-ranking field officers, and about that many of their village politicians. They were fit to be tied. Finally the northmen had to come outta their holes. Losing face, see, to a lousy six-man team. They sprung their trap on us at Vanh Duc—and of course, that's what we'd been aiming at all the time. We got a full battalion chasing our butts out across the rice paddies, and that's where they met our air force."

"I remember that operation," Harrington put in. "That was the time the airborne infantry was living in helicopters for three days."

"That was Vanh Duc," Zitka confirmed, nodding his head soberly. "We smoked 'em out, and what the air force didn't get, the Ninth did."

"We're playing a Vanh Duc game here," Bolan explained. He glanced at his watch. "Only there will be no air-force or infantry reinforcements to finish the job once we've smoked the enemy into the open. We have to do the entire job ourselves. We're going to hit 'em, and hit 'em, and keep on hitting 'em until they're trying to hide up each other's asses. Then, when we know who they are and where they are, all of them—then we squash them. That's the entire plan. We play the details by ear. Gadgets has bugs all over Giordano's house, and he put a recorder on the telephone. In just about two hours, Zitter and Bloodbrother will take up their stakeout positions. Flower, you're on Zitter. Gunsmoke, on Bloodbrother. You know the routing—play it like life and death, 'cause that's what it's going to be. Boom, you alternate the electronics watch with some Gadgets. Politician and Deadeye, on me but not too close, give me room to operate. Chopper, you've got base camp security. Oh—and Boom, how long would it take you to make about a dozen of those little impact grenades?"

"You don't want fragmentation?" the explosives man asked solemnly.

"No. Just plenty of flash and concussion."

"Hell—twenty minutes," Hoffower replied.

"Good. Do it now. Put them in a hip pouch for me." Bolan smiled and got to his feet. "This is going to be a lot better than Pittsfield. I'm glad you people are with me." He started to walk away, then checked his stride and turned back with an afterthought. "Oh—Politician has the money divvied up into eleven shares. It figured to forty-seven-fifty per man. The eleventh share is for the kitty. Pick up your money and then get some rest. There won't be much sleeping tonight." He turned abruptly and strode off the patio, heading for the beach.

"What's this bitty about the kitty?" Andromede asked, addressing no one in particular.

"The war fund," Blancanales explained. "Told me to put his share in there too."

"Somebody loan me three hundred," Fontenelli said. He was the first at the table and was fingering a packet of bills with reverence. "I wanta know what five grand feels like, all in one hunk."

"Where's he going?" Hoffower asked, gazing after the departing leader.

Zitka picked up his share of the spoils and said quietly, "He always goes off by himself for a while after a strike. Leave 'im alone."

"If he don't want the money, what *does* he want?" Hoffower persisted.

"Aw hell, Boom, they rubbed out his whole family," Harrington said.

"It's a holy war," Andromede murmured. "The Karmic pattern. The law of retribution. Liberation from hell to heaven—and maybe back to hell again."

Hoffower was carefully counting his stack of bills. He thrust a wad at Blancanales. "Here's the thousand he advanced me," he said quietly. "Put it in the kitty."

"It wasn't an advance," Blancanales protested. "It's a bonus."

"Put it in the kitty anyway," Hoffower insisted.

36

Blancanales accepted the money and added it to the stack on the table. Andromede stared at the "war fund" for a strained moment, then quickly counted a thousand dollars from his packet and dropped it onto the table. Fontenelli wavered painfully, then followed suit.

Washington was staring after the quickly receding figure of Mack Bolan as he trudged up the beach. "There go de judge," he said with a soft sigh. Then he stepped to the table and deposited a stack of bills.

Loudelk was smiling faintly. "Soft probe, eh?" He tossed an uncounted stack into the growing kitty. "Here's my vote for the winning side."

The vote of confidence quickly became unanimous, the war fund swelled, and—most important—the *ten* had become *one*.

Flower Child Andromede walked to the edge of the patio, then turned back to his comrades, his face in a saintly expression, and said, "Vanh Duc, Vanh Duc, through blood and muck, if it's not a gangbang, it's a piece of bad luck."

"What he talking about?" Washington muttered.

"Liberation, I guess," Loudelk quietly replied. "We know about that bag, don't we, black man?"

Washington grinned without humor. "Yeah, man, we know that bag." He raised his voice and directed it toward Andromede. "Hey, Chaplain—come on over here and confess my sins."

"You handle your sins, brother, and I'll handle mine," Andromede replied, grinning. "Right now, I go to build up my contempt of death. Join me. We'll meditate together beside the still waters."

"I'll join you at Vanh Duc, man," Washington replied softly.

"There's a reality." Andromede sighed and walked away. Death, he had long ago decided, was the only true reality.

Chapter Four

HARDCASE

Captain Tim Braddock had been with the Los
Angeles Police for eighteen years. Married, father
of three, still hard and trim at the age of forty-two,
he looked more the successful young business ex-
ecutive than a captain of detectives. Braddock was
"on his way," according to the scuttlebutt around
the Hall of Justice. Respected, admired, compe-
tent, effective—these were the terms most com-
monly employed in any discussion of the man. For
the previous two years, he had been shunted into
administrative and liaison details, public-relations
work, and other nonpolicing duties that seemed to
be pointing him toward higher echelons of police
business. And now he had been assigned as coordinator of the hottest job to hit the force since the
Kennedy assassination—the Bolan case.

The project had been appropriately code named
Hardcase. It had aroused the active interest of every police agency in the state. Representatives of
most of these were now assembling in the briefing
room to hear L.A.'s approach to the problem. A
man from the Attorney General's office in Sacramento would be out there, as would liaison men
from the state troopers, several federal agencies,
and various sheriff's departments and a heavy con-
tingent from L.A.'s neighboring municipalities.

Braddock felt as though he were about to enter
a lineup; in just a moment he would be asked to
step forward, stand straight, state his name and
occupation, and say something in his natural
voice. He shivered inwardly. A forlorn part of him
wished fervently for a return to the earlier, simpler,

no-nonsense days of cops and robbers, to a time when being a cop was simply being a bastard, going after the lawbreaker, and shooting him dead or bringing him in to a certain punishment. The practical area of Braddock's mind knew, however, that those simple old days were gone forever. A cop was now one part politician, one part diplomat, one part big brother, one part father image, one part savant, one part constitutional lawyer— all of which left very little room for that part which was just plain cop.

The "just plain cop" was a vanishing American. Tim Braddock did not wish to vanish. He had come a long distance in eighteen years; eighteen more might well see him sitting at the big desk in the chief's office. Ambition could be a stern taskmaster; in this twentieth-century pressure-boiler world of competition, the will to succeed was closely akin to the instinct for survival. It boiled down to that, and no one was more aware of this grim fact than was Tim Braddock.

He squelched the butterflies flitting about his stomach with a stern inner command and listened as the deputy chief was introduced, then allowed his mind to wander as the number-two at L.A. made his presentation of the broad generalities of the case. Braddock was well acquainted with the generalities. He was certain that every officer in the room was equally aware of The Executioner's background and recent history. The audience was respectfully attentive, however; after all Braddock reasoned, the man addressing them was merely one step below the top of the largest police agency west of Chicago. Also, they were being asked for neither approval nor cooperation. Braddock, in his talk, would be asking for both. There would be no room, at that podium, for just-plain-cop Tim Braddock. And if he did not pull this thing properly . . .

well, that chief's desk would begin to look mighty remote.

The deputy chief was angling into Braddock's introduction. ". . . And Captain Braddock will be coordinating this department's handling of the Bolan affair. His office will be the point of direct contact between all local, state, and federal efforts toward Hardcase. Gentlemen—Captain Tim Braddock, Los Angeles Police Department."

Someone in the back of the room applauded briefly as Braddock walked toward the podium. Applause was out of order here. The captain tossed a wink at the back wall, smiled drolly, and spoke into the microphone. "*Some*body out there knows me," he said genially.

The audience responded with light laughter and Braddock's guts felt better. The ice was broken. "Just so that *every*body will know me, Officer John Ward will distribute some cards." He angled a nod toward a uniformed officer who stood in the pit just below the speaker's platform. "You can think of these as calling cards," Braddock went on, in the lightly genial manner he preferred for starters. "I'd appreciate it, though, if you would regard the information on these cards as confidential. The telephone numbers you'll find there are reserved exclusively for Hardcase communications. The radio frequencies are for special primary and secondary nets established for mobile units assigned to Hardcase. We presently have ten cars assigned exclusively to this project on a twenty-four-hour basis. Each car is assigned to a specific sector of the city. We are going to ask that each of our neighboring police agencies maintain a listening watch on these special nets, so that they may be fully on top of any developments and be prepared to lend assistance as required."

Officer Ward was moving efficiently along the

line of chairs, issuing a stack of the cards to be passed along each row. Braddock continued. "Special instructions have been issued to every mobile unit in this department, for a prearranged reaction upon receipt of a Hardcase alert. Bolan is a military tactician, and a darned effective one, I'm told. He should not be regarded as a lunatic. He is not a wild-eyed fanatic or a bloodthirsty gunslinger, and any attempts to deal with him from this viewpoint will generally be ineffective. From all I have been able to learn of his M.O., he studiously avoids any confrontation with police authority. He apparently goes to great lengths to protect innocent bystanders. He is still, of course, a dangerous criminal. He must be apprehended at the earliest possible moment.

"Now—I want to take just a moment to review with you The Executioner's activities at Pittsfield last month."

Braddock shuffled his papers, delicately cleared his throat, directed a pleasant gaze upon the assemblage, then began his reading. "On August 22nd, firing from an upper floor of a building a hundred yards distant, he shot to death five officers of a Mafia-controlled loan company, in the street outside their office. He used a Marlin .444 with telescopic sights, and he fired only five shots. There was no return fire, although two of his victims were armed. No injuries were sustained by bystanders.

"Apparently he then managed to infiltrate the local Mafia activities, went to work for them, and gained a familiarity with their operations in and around Pittsfield. According to police intelligence, the Mafia was tipped to Bolan's true role shortly thereafter, and a contract was let for his death. On the morning of August•31st, two Murder, Incor-

41

porated, contractors were shot to death during a gun battle in Bolan's apartment.

"This is when the fireworks began in earnest, and this is where the Bolan M.O. begins to show its sting. He seems to go in for the thunder-and-lightning technique, hitting hard, fast, and repeatedly in a blitzkrieg offensive which keeps his enemies reeling and confused. On the afternoon of August 31st, Bolan knocked over a prize pleasure palace . . ." Braddock raised his eyes and grinned. "A house of prostitution, gentlemen." A responsive titter from the assembled lawmen greeted the unnecessary explanation.

Braddock paused to allow the good humor to run its course; then he continued. "He knocked over a prized palace in a suburban community, burning it to the ground, then lay cooly on a distant hillock and shot the tires off a parked police cruiser and a fire captain's car, then punched a fusillade into an approaching carload of Mafia henchmen, wounding one of them severely and destroying the expensive automobile."

A shuffling and chuckling in the audience again brought Braddock to a pause. He dabbed at his forehead with a handerchief. "It's no wonder this boy captured the public fancy," he went on. "A lot of people identified with him, you see, even a lot of police officers. This is an attitude that has worked in Bolan's favor. Needless to say, it hurts the police efforts. Bolan is a war hero. He has been repeatedly decorated for valor and heroism. Many honest, law-abiding citizens are in strong sympathy with him. The Bolan image runs somewhat along these lines: One of our boys in Vietnam, a decorated boy, is called home from the wars to bury his family, victims of Mafia terrorism. Heroic boy from Vietnam becomes avenger, declares a one-man war on the homefront underworld, and sallies forth into a heroic war against another of our country's enemies. Bunk!"

Braddock raised his eyes to gaze levelly upon his audience. "I say again, gentlemen—*bunk!* This is a terribly and a dangerously misleading image. Mack Bolan is a highly trained death machine. He is extremely dangerous, both in a positive and in a negative sense. He is a remorseless killer, an *executioner* in the strictest sense, a brilliant tactician who would replace law and justice with the code of the battlefield. He is judge and jury, prosecution and defense, the law, the final word.

"But let's get back to Pittsfield. A short while after his assault upon the pleasure palace, he shows up at the palatial estate of one of the Mafia chieftains. He is dressed in a power-company uniform. He coldbloodedly slips a knife into the two security men guarding the property and dumps their bodies into the swimming pool, after first severing power and telephone lines and luring the men out of the house to 'assist' him in checking out the trouble. Then he goes inside the house, slashes the mattresses on all the beds, and shoots up a large portrait of the Mafia chieftain. This was purely a harrassment tactic—obviously he knew that the owner of the property was not at home.

"But this is another significant feature of the Bolan M.O. Apparently he had been exposed before he could penetrate into the higher councils of the Mafia. He was trying to jar them, frighten them— to roust them into a panic that would smoke the higher ups into the open. And this boy does move fast. Listen, now. That same afternoon he returned to the scene of his first hit, the loan company, calmly walked in and helped himself to a secret Mafia cache of undeclared wealth, some one-quarter million, it is said, then ordered the employees to stack all their loan records in a pile on the floor and burn them."

Braddock looked up with a broad grin. "Now, how many thousands of good, upstanding citizens would you imagine became endeared to The Executioner through that simple act? He burned the loan records."

Again he waited for the amused response to settle; then he continued. "I'm trying to give you some insight into this guy—and possibly explain why the news people have contributed so much to his hero image. He *is* a heroic figure. He's a natural for the role. People enjoy hearing about a guy who is getting away with it, especially if they can visualize him wearing a clean white hat.

"It should be noted, also, that Bolan apparently has an appreciation for his image. He picks his battlefields carefully, confining them, generally, to Mafia property. He is kind and considerate to bystanders and goes to great lengths to keep them out of the line of fire. Instead of bursting into a house with his guns blazing, he meticulously weeds out the villains, invites them outside, and neatly dispatches them. A household servant does not even see the color of their blood.

"That night—that same night, yes; he keeps moving—Bolan broke contact at another chieftain's house and ran when the guy's wife starts plinking away at him with a little target pistol. He did not return her fire but elected to break off and run, and it cost him. He was hit, but I guess not too badly. He dropped out of sight for a few days. He could afford to. Earlier that same evening, the night he was wounded, he had followed one of the chieftains to a Mafia family council and broke up the proceedings with a long-range sniper attack—and this one seemed calculated to only serve notice that he had located their

44

headquarters. This is another M.O.-significant tactic. He tied it in later. The family's nerves must have been fraying tremendously during Bolan's recuperative period. Even the fates, it seems, are sympathetic with this guy.

"Follow this action, now, in his second blitzkrieg. First he calls the local police department and warns them that he's hitting tonight—and to keep clear. Is he naive, brazen, or boastful?" Braddock shook his head. "Apparently his first stop is at a private warehouse where war-surplus munitions and arms are kept. Note the image keeping, now. He breaks into the warehouse and carefully selects a personal arsenal. He leaves behind a detail itemization of the stolen goods—and more than enough money to pay for them.

"And now, on to the blitzkrieg. A series of lightning strikes, at widely separated locations, succeeds in bringing the local Mafia hierarchy into full session. It appears that they committed themselves to a full and final confrontation, and the forces they had arrayed against this man were formidable, to say the least. Bolan must have known that he was walking into a Mafia setup. Of course he knew—he had maneuvered them into just such a confrontation. And the Pittsfield family never really understood the Bolan mentality. He'd been fighting them all along with conventional weapons. A knife, a pistol, a high-powered rifle. He was a man alone. The Mafia brought in a small army, set up some machine guns, and thought they would squash him like a bug the minute he made his move. He showed them the error of their thinking, and we certainly have to respect the Bolan fighting brain. He hit those people with everything in the arsenal, and he was waging a war like the soldier he is. He lit the skies with flares, then sat safely in the dark, a quarter mile away, and hit them with mortars, rockets, and—you name it, he had it. The most amazing part of this entire incredible story is that he then slipped through a police dragnet that numbered more than a hundred city and county lawmen."

Braddock cleared his throat and dropped his voice a pitch to observe, "It would seem safe to conclude that not every lawman in that dragnet was overly anxious to apprehend The Executioner. Not because of cowardice—because of admiration, perhaps even affection. Somebody turned his head the other way as Bolan was passing by. Bet on it." Braddock mopped his forehead with a handkerchief and continued in his normal voice, "So now we have the problem here. Bolan has brought his war to Los Angeles County. There was a gunfight last week at a residence club out near the beach. When the smoke cleared, six hoods who have been identified as murder contractors lay dead in a parking lot directly adjacent to a patio party where some forty young people were relaxing and enjoying life. It was a miracle that none of these innocents were hit by that spray of bullets. We have since learned that one of the tenants of that building, one George K. Zitka, is a Vietnam veteran and a friend of Mack Bolan. Zitka, need I add, has dropped from sight.

"Yesterday morning, one of the most exclusive neighborhoods of this area was rocked by a Bolan-type strike that left two dead and a known Mafia figure terrorized. It has been definitely established that at least a half dozen men were with Bolan on this hit.

"Keep in mind, now—in Pittsfield, Bolan was alone, and look at the trail of carnage he left in and about the city. He is now in Los Angeles—and he is no longer a man alone. He has a gang now, and these people are apparently conducting mili-

46

tary-type operations against certain elements of this community."

Braddock paused dramatically, smiled, and said, "I have not come to praise the Mafia—nor even to bury them." The audience tittered. "My heart does not bleed for 'Melio Giordano, nor for the two thugs who were rather dramatically chopped from his payroll. But my blood runs cold at the thought of an organized gang war in this city. You all know the certain results of gunfights in our city's streets. We cannot have it. We simply *will not* have it."

The room had become very quiet. Braddock paused to sip at a tumbler of water. He had their full attention. Now to sell them. "It is common knowledge that a six-figure open contract has been let, with Mack Bolan's name on the death warrant. Already, since the publicity of yesterday's strike, twenty-two out-of-town gunmen have been spotted and picked up for questioning. We are being invaded by the most vicious criminal elements from around the nation. Oh, we're picking them up. Just as fast as we can identify them, we pick them up. But it's like a grunion run. For each one we grab, ten slip through our fingers. Gentlemen, Los Angeles County has been invaded by every ambitious gunman in the country. They will shoot at anything that looks like Mack Bolan. There's the negative danger of Bolan's presence in this city. Sudden death can erupt on any street or in any public place or in any private residence in this city and county. We have to get Bolan. We have to get him *quickly*."

Okay, he had them. They were listening, and they were believing. Rally 'round the flag, boys, the heat is on, Let's sew this guy up good and get him on ice and out of our hair. This was Braddock's message. He would get it across.

"Now we have stakeouts on every known Mafia figure in the area. There are not many—and we think our intelligence is as good as Bolan's. Just to make sure, we are shaking the city good, double checking our informants and then checking them again. Giordano's name was on the Attorney General's list. Possibly Bolan is using that same list. We don't want to make things so tight that we scare Bolan off, of course. And we certainly do not wish to engage him in a shootout, not until we have maneuvered him onto a battlefield of *our* choosing. Therefore, here is the strategy we are using for Hardcase."

Braddock stepped over to a large chart on the wall behind him and picked up a pointer. "We are asking your fullest cooperation in this strategy. All right. We form a loose circle around the probable points of contact, and we play the waiting game. At any time when contact is made, we tighten the circle slightly, set up our net of containment, and run him to ground only when that ground is not likely to get drenched with the blood of innocent citizens. Remember—we are chasing what now appears to be a small but highly professional army. They have heavy weapons. These people will undoubtedly stand and fight if it seems that arrest is imminent. We do not want that fight to spill out upon innocent citizens. We ask that all adjacent communities cooperate fully with us in this plan. We ask the right of 'hot pursuit' into other police jurisdictions. We ask that the utmost delicacy be exercised in every phase of Hardcase and that . . ."

Braddock was not really asking now—he was telling. A seasoned instinct had signalled that the time was ripe for him to assume command of this motley assortment of lawmen. All the other parts of himself had become exhausted as he maneuvered into the minds of those cops out there—

now, just-plain-cop Tim Braddock was in the saddle and riding hard. He would get this guy Bolan, or by God there would be no other kind of cop left in him. His cool stare lifted out over the heads of California's finest as he thumped the chart here and there with the pointer to exphasize certain points, and not a man seated there possessed the slightest doubt that The Executioner would meet his fate in Los Angeles.

"Big Tim" Braddock was a man on his way. A dozen Mack Bolans would not stand in that way. The heat was on, Big Tim was stoking the boiler, and it could not be said with any certainty whether Hardcase described the operation or the man who was directing it. In either event, the heat was on. Hardcase was set.

Chapter Five

THE TRACK

Emilio Giordano would not be any man's funny bunny. Only once during his thirty years of manhood had any man made a monkey out of him, and that man had died quickly and violently. Not once during the past fifteen years had any man spoken to him in disrespectful tones, except that stupid senator on the crime commission and that ignorant Sacramento lump they called an Attorney General—and both of these were now smarting under the lash of unrelenting political pressures. If a damn dumb sergeant—a deserter, at that—a common thief and gunman thought *he* could make Emilio Giordano roll over and play funny bunny for him, then by the blood of Saint Matthew that damn dumb sergeant was going to die with a Giordano grapefruit up his ass.

Fifteen years had passed since 'Milio had last worn a gun. He still knew how to use one. Yeah. Some things a man never loses, like his touch with a fine pistol. He inspected the shiny .38, took a couple of familiarity pulls on the trigger, then loaded it and stuffed it into the holster on the backside of his hip. Next he withdrew his wallet and shuffled through an assortment of cards until he found the gun permit, checked the expiration date, then carefully inserted the permit into a prominent display envelope and returned the wallet to his pocket. No dumb moves by 'Milio, like packing hardware without a license. Hell no.

"Take it easy," Varone had advised him, when Giordano called him earlier that afternoon. Sure. Take it easy. Play funny bunny. Let the miserable dumbhead tie you to a manure heap. And rob you. And walk all over you like you're not 'Milio Giordano, Il Fortunato, in whose blood rages four generations of Maffio. Take it easy? Emilio Giordano would *never* take it *that* easy.

"He wants you to play his game," Varone had said. "Can't you see what he's doing? He wants you to run scared and do something stupid. Now don't play his game. Don't play, 'Milio."

Well, 'Millio *would* play. He would play the game. But not dumbhead's game. He would show the sergeant a game or two.

Giordano moved around his desk and depressed an intercom button. A fluttery male voice responded immediately. "You got the money, Jerry?" Giordano asked.

"Yes sir. Twenty-five thousand. Twenties and fifties."

"All right, bring it up. No—meet me out back. Right now."

Giordano broke the connection and thumbed down another station. "Hey!" he barked. "Wake up out there!"

"Yessir—garage," came a crisp reply.

"You got the cars ready?"

"Yessir. We're ready."

"Awright. I'm coming down. Keep your eyes open, dammit."

"Yessir, we're doing that."

Giordano grunted and strode out of his study and through the back of the house. He could hear the carpenters banging noisily in his bedroom, upstairs, and this renewed his irritation with "the dumbhead." He kicked the rear door as he opened it and pounded on the handrail of the stairway with an open palm as he quickly descended to the yard.

A gleaming black-and-chrome Continental occupied the driveway. Five of his best boys were in it, conversing in low tones. The driver waved with his fingers as Giordano strode past and received a slow wink in return.

Il Fortunato stepped into a sparkling white Rolls-Royce and seated himself beside a younger man on whose lap reposed a square black briefcase. The two men up front, in the chauffeur's compartment, wore uniforms of unrelieved black, but white chauffeur's caps with gold braid across the visors. Giordano depressed an intercom button on the armrest and said, "Danny, go back and make sure Bruno understands two minutes."

The uniformed man who was seated beside the driver jerked his head in understanding, stepped out of the Rolls, carefully closed the door, and walked quickly into the garage. Another Continental waited in there, carrying a rear guard of another five men.

"He wants to be sure you understand the two-minute wait before you take off," Danny reported.

A lean young man in the front seat nodded his head curtly. "Christ, yeah, we understand," he replied in obvious disgust. "And in case he's wondering, we got the route, too. Santa Ana freeway to the Riverside cutoff and then, dammit, there ain't any other way to get there."

Danny smiled and returned to the Rolls. He began his report through the thick glass, then remembered, depressed the intercom button, and said, "They're all set, Mr. Giordano."

"They understand they don't leave here for two minutes?" Giordano snapped.

"Yes sir, two minutes, they understand."

"Dumbheads probably don't even know the route."

"Yes sir, Santa Ana Freeway to the cutoff, then the blacktop to the rear gate. They understand."

"Awright," Giordano growled. "Let's go check on our grapefruit."

The chauffeur tapped his horn lightly. The lead Continental moved smoothly along the drive, and the Rolls eased along after it. Giordano settled back into the protection of armor plating and bulletproof glass. Don't play, eh? By God, 'Milio was going to play. And the dumbhead was going to *pay*.

Deadeye Washington slid hastily down the grassy slope, heavy binoculars strapped about his neck, and called out, "Okay, they just left. Two cars. Big black one in front, Lincoln or something, and a big white limousine, two chauffeurs, man. Sure making it easy to track."

Bolan smiled tightly and slipped a jaunty plaid beret onto his head. "Maybe two *damn* easy," he said. He leaned into the Corvette and came out with a compact two-way radio. "Trackers," he announced into the mouthpiece, "Eagle says they're loose." Bolan glanced at Washington.

The Negro mouthed the word, "Bloodbrother."

Bolan nodded and continued the announcement without interruption. "One rich Detroit black, one white millionaire close behind, on Track Two."

Loudelk's soft voice purred back immediately. "Affirm. Passing Track Two . . . right . . . now! Track Two now on quarry. Here's the count. Five in Detroit black. Four in big English white tank, repeat, tank. Track Two on target and going away fast."

Zitka's clipped tones leaped in. "Roj, roj, Track One going 'round for pickup at Point Delta."

"Track on loose," Bolan commanded. "It smells, repeat, smells."

A faint "Wilco" came in from Loudelk, followed by a loud retort from Zitka. "Bluesuits on," he yelped. "Tearing toward Track Two. Beware, beware."

"Affirm, Track Two is being wary," replied the cautious Indian voice.

"Close only on signal!" Bolan commanded. He laid the radio on the seat of the Corvette and slid in behind the wheel, made a sign with his fingers to Washington, and spun the little car about in a jouncing circle, then hit the pavement and sped down the hill.

Washington was sprinting toward an idling Mustang parked in a shelter of trees some yards off the street. He climbed in on the passenger's side, rolled his eyes toward Blancanales, and panted, "Okay. Keep 'im in sight."

The Mustang leaped forward. Washington braced himself with his feet and swung the binoculars into the rear seat, lifted the corner of a blanket, shoved a clip into the long Mauser, and settled back with a sigh.

"Bloodbrother says they got a tank," he reported.

Blancanales was whipping the Mustang along the curving downgrade. He raised an eyebrow and said, "Yeah?"

"Yeah. Must be one o' them tailor-made bulletproof jobs. Just looked like a big white limousine to me, through the glasses."

"Sounds like it's going to be a ball."

"You don't know nothing yet. Sarge smells an ambush, and Zitter says cops has joined the parade."

"I take it we're trailing loose, then," Blancanales observed. His right hand fumbled on the seat for the radio. He thrust it at Washington. "You'll have to stick the antenna out the window," he instructed. "Find out what the hell we're doing."

The radio became operational just in time for them to hear Bolan's voice command, "Flanks, report in. Flanks."

"Flander Two here," Gunsmoke Harrington

54

drawled. "Flanker One also. We're together and following the play in the Horse."

Blancanales nodded his silent approval. "Good," he whispered.

Bolan was replying, "You're not in sight. Where do you run?"

"We run starboard to track. Will join up at straightaway."

Washington grinned. "Sounds like a Dixie Horserace," he snorted.

"That horse is too conspicuous up here," Blancanales muttered. "But it'll blend in okay on the freeway."

"What if we don't take the freeway?" Washington wondered aloud.

"Doesn't everybody?"

Bolan was now replying, following a brief silence on the radio. "Okay, Flank. Good thinking. Track one, position report."

"Track One is right on bluesuits," Zitka snapped back.

"Are they in official vehicle?"

"Neg, neg. Plainjanes, brown Pontiac. But they're fuzzy, no mistake."

Another brief silence, then: "Okay, and another parader is right on *you*, buddy-o. Now who the hell?"

They could hear Zitka's carrier wave idling for several seconds before his voice clipped in. "I dunno, but it's a big black and it's got a five count."

"Uh-huh, that's great," Bolan said. "It figures—a delayed rear guard. Okay, Break away, Track One, with caution, and come around on me."

"Roj. Approaching straightaway now. I'll make my move up there."

"Track Two is on station and maintaining," Loudelk reported. "Instructions!"

"Maintain track!" Bolan snapped.

"Affirm."

Blancanales and Washington exchanged solemn glances. They had a good view now of the fiery Corvette ahead. In the distance, they could see the ramp rising to the freeway and the white limousine ascending. Washington craned about to inspect the road behind; then he pressed the transmitter button and spoke into the radio. "Backboard. It's clear to the rear," he reported.

"Roger, Backboard," Bolan replied. "Flanker—I believe I have you in sight now. Can you identify bluesuiter?"

"Brown Pontiac? 'Firmative. One, two, uh, three up off you, Maestro. The field is getting thick, though."

"Yeah. Uh . . . can you safely detain them?"

"Not without getting detained myself. Unless you want 'em zipped."

"Hell no, no zipping!" Bolan replied. "Intercept. Repeat, intercept and delay only."

"Gotcha," Harrinton said. "Will intercept on straightaway. Can somebody help us build a box?"

Zitka's voice chimed in, "I'm natural for that. During my breakaway. Okay, Maestro?"

"Affirmative," Bolan said. "Play it cool. Arouse no suspicion."

"Roj."

The Mustang was climbing the ramp now, Blancanales tensing at the wheel to merge into the swiftly moving traffic of the freeway. The Corvette swerved across two lanes, accelerating in a fullthroated power shift. Blancanales swung in moments later, several cars behind and in the outside lane. He watched his rear view cautiously, then angled across to the inside lane, picking up speed and interlaning to regain position on Bolan's rear. As they headed into a long curve, Washington muttered, "I think I see the horse up there, 'bout mid-curve. Isn't that it? Outside lane?"

Blancanales was hunched over the steering wheel and squinting through the windshield. "Looks like it," he replied. "How'd they get so far ahead?"

"Musta come down the perimeter, got on ahead of us," Washington surmised.

Harrington's voice crackled through the radio at that moment, confirming the tentative indentification. "We're leading the parade," he reported. "Have the grand marshal in view, coming up on my rear, middle lane, big Detroit black, English white right behind. I'm starting to throttle back. Get set for that box, Tracker."

"I'm moving up," Bolan announced. "Hold the box until I'm through. Backboard, where the hell are you?"

"Right in your blind spot, Maestro," Washington reported.

"Okay, all units except Tracker Two, we'll all join the box and try for a grand slam. Listen carefully, there's only time for this once, so get it straight the first time around. Number the lanes 1, 2, 3, and 4—left to right. The interchange is about three minutes away. Lane 4 leaves us there and swings toward the Harbor. Quarry is holding steady in Lane 2, my guess is for either the Santa Ana or the San Berdue. All right, here are positions. Backboard, you come up on my . . ."

Washington was listening to Bolan's calm instructions with a feeling of vague unreality. It just did not seem for real. Here they were, barreling along the damn Hollywood Freeway at better than a mile a minute, practically bumper to bumper in an endless stream of cars moving four abreast, on ramps and off ramps looming up in an almost monotonous recurrence, and in all this, Bolan was

57

trying to set up a traffic trap for two of those hurtling objects. He shook his head and glanced at Blancanales. His partner was listening attentively to the instructions, his eyes flicking in an endless circle, right, left, dead ahead, into the mirror, right, left ... It made Washington feel a bit light headed.

"Okay, Horse," Bolan was saying, "start your move. Drop down to fifty ... good ... good ... one minute to interchange ..."

Washington saw the red Corvette squirt across two lanes of traffic and weave back into their lane several positions ahead. A huge van semitrailer, the vehicle referred to as the horse, was laboring along just ahead, in the far right lane. Three cars that had been following the horse reacted to its sudden slowing by whipping into the second outboard lane and passing. Washington caught a glimpse of the vehicle that was maintaining the "hole" between the two lanes of traffic—it was Bolan's Corvette. He grinned. The two cars now between Bolan and Blancanales were the police vehicle, first, and the third Mafia car. The driver of the Continental was beginning to cast anxious glances to his left and right. Washington could visualize what was going to happen next, and his grin broadened.

"Backboard, on station!" Bolan commanded.

Blancanales stomped the accelerator and whipped the Mustang into Lane 3, pulled quickly abreast of Bolan, and stayed there.

"Okay—Zitter."

The Mercury wagon being piloted by Zitka moved almost sideways into the extreme inboard lane, and now the four of them—Zitka, Blancanales, Bolan, and the diesel horse—were pacing the traffic into the interchange at a leisurely fifty miles per hour.

The next few moments were tense ones and would have proved less anxious if one more vehicle had been available to maintain a two-car gap directly behind the horse. Split-second timing had made the insurance unnecessary, however, and they glided into the boxing zone with the trap perfectly set. The police car, seeing daylight between Bolan and the horse, and with the Giordano vehicle rapidly disappearing into the interchange, whipped over suddenly behind the horse. A puff of smoke belched from the twin exhausts as the Pontiac's passing gear kicked in and it leaned toward the hole between Bolan's right front fender and the left rear corner of the van.

The Mafia rear-guard Continental had swung into the Pontiac's wake, with the obvious intention of following right on through the slot. The slot, however, suddenly ceased to exist as Bolan eased forward with his front bumper directly abreast the horse's rear wheels.

Washington caught a fleeting glimpse of an infuriated face behind the wheel of the police car as tires squealed and the heavy car lurched back into position behind the horse, brakes grabbing in the abrupt forced slowdown. Washington heard but did not see the Continental smack the rear of the police car. It was a light tap, accompanied by more squealing of tires and the sounds of crunching metal and shattering glass.

The horse was now curving gracefully onto the cloverleaf, the two vehicles following in jerky confusion. The vehicles of the Death Squad, less horse, picked up speed and hurried to close on the quarry.

Bolan's elated voice came through the radio: "Beautiful, beautiful—that's playing it by the numbers."

"That's playing it by your quivering ass," Zitka shot back.

"Playing, hell," Harrington sang in. "Where the hell am I headed? How do I get this big sunabitch back on the track?"

"Follow the cloverleaf on around," Bolan snapped back. "Just follow the signs and come on around. We're taking the . . . yeah, the Santa Ana. Rejoin with all possible speed. How did our friends make out?"

Harrington was chuckling into the radio. "They're out of the game. Locked bumpers, looks like. Madder . . . than . . . *hell!*"

"Better than we hoped for," Bolan replied. "Okay—good show, boys. Resume positions and tally-ho."

Washington grinned at Blancanales and shook his head. "Hell, this is some damn outfit, isn't it?" he commented quietly.

Blancanales nodded as he fell into formation several positions behind the Corvette. Zitka's Mercury was burning rubber up the inside lane to close on Loudelk.

"Light me a cigarette," Blancanales requested. "I'm afraid to take my hand off the wheel. I'm afraid it'll shake off at the shoulder."

Washington guffawed, lit the cigarette, and shoved it between his partner's lips. "Yeah, man, it's some damn outfit," he repeated. "Sure glad I joined up. How 'bout you?"

"Just wait," Blancanales murmured. "Do you know how close we came to having a twenty-jillion-car smashup?"

The big Negro was grinning merrily. "Wait for what, man?"

"Wait 'till we finish this mission. If I'm still alive then . . . well, yeah—I guess I'm glad I'm in."

"If you're dead, man, you won't know the difference. You better be glad now, while you got time."

Blancanales flashed his companion a sudden smile. "You're right," he siad. "It's a hell of a squad."

Chapter Six

THE AMBUSH AT THE BUTTES

"Has that station wagon been behind us all the way or hasn't it?" queried the nervous young man with the briefcase.

"Off and on, sure he has," Giordano replied smugly. "You just now catching on?"

"Well, I thought at first . . . well, there was this Ford sedan back there for a while, and now the station wagon is back. It looks like the same one."

Giordano chuckled and slumped contentedly into the plush upholstery. "Games," he said. "They like to play games. Okay. Let 'em play."

They had left the freeway some minutes earlier and were powering smoothly through gently lifting countryside on a smooth blacktop road, the big cars eating the pavement at a steady eighty-mile-per-hour clip. Soon they would drop onto the desert-like flats bordering the city of Riverside and swing north into the rocky buttes. Giordano's groves lay in there, in a sheltered valley between the stark rock formations. Grapefruit, lemons, tangerines, and avocados were grown there, but hardly in sufficient quantity to support the rich Giordano appetites. Actually, the groves had proved to be an excellent deduction for income-tax purposes; Giordano made money by losing money in his farming operation. As a legitimate business venture, the farm was a minor item in the varied Giordano interests, but it tied in neatly with his more secretive activities, serving as a sort of central clearing house for an underworld empire.

The Rolls was slowing for the turn onto the backroad approach to the groves. Giordano frowned and punched the intercom button. "What happened to our hide-and-seek pals?" he growled.

"He kept falling back," the driver reported. "Lost sight of him about a mile back."

"Pull onto the back road and stop," Giordano commanded.

They made the turn. The heavy car came to a smooth halt. The black Continental proceeded on for several hundred feet, then halted also and backed down to within a few yards of the Rolls.

"Keep your eyes open," Giordano snapped. "Dumbhead can't even play hide and seek. Soon as you see him coming, start up again, but *slow*. We don't want him to lose us."

The driver poked his head out the window and shouted instructions to the car ahead. They waited. Giordano chafed. He lit a cigar after several minutes and growled, "Dumbhead! *Dumb*head! How could he lose us on a country road?"

"Maybe he had car trouble," the young man ventured.

"Aaagh! So where the hell is Bruno! Eh? Where the hell is Bruno?" He punched the intercom button. "So where the hell is brilliant Bruno, who knows the goddamn route, eh?"

"Someone's coming up!" the driver announced.

Giordano's head snapped to the window. He squinted down the road they had left minutes earlier, then made a disgusted sound deep in his throat. "A truck! A goddamn truck!"

A huge blue-and-white diesel van was sweeping up the road toward their position, a thin column of dark smoke ejecting from the overhead exhaust. Giordano watched its approach, his disgust growing. Two men were in the cab. As it thundered by, the driver sounded a salute on his air horn.

"Some ambush," Giordano muttered. "Two

63

dumbheads. One can't even play tag, and the other can't remember the route two times in a row." He punched the intercom button. "Awright, go on. Go on, go on!"

Bolan had fallen off into a leisurely forty-mile-per-hour advance moments after leaving the freeway. Blancanales had remained at the cutoff to await the horse, which was several minutes behind.

"Heading into my kind of country," Loudelk had reported. "Good place for a hit."

"Play it cool," Bolan instructed. "Rotate the track."

"Okay. I'm falling back. Come on up, Zit."

"Roj. Those bastards must be doing ninety. This old wagon is shaking apart."

"Just eighty," Loudelk reported. "Can't you overtake me? I'm dropping off to seventy . . . sixty. You'll have to push ninety, Zit, or you'll lose them."

"I'm doin' a flat hunnert right now!"

Bolan grinned and stayed out of it.

"Bye-bye, Birdie," Loudelk sang a moment later. "You're looking great. Hang in there, white eyes."

"Okay." Zitka's voice was strained with excitement. "I have them in sight. Don't get too far behind, Brother. Those cats are flat moving out."

"Affirm. What's that up there on the left? Buttes?"

"Yeah." Moments later: "Uh-oh. There's a fork up here. They're swinging north, into the buttes."

Bolan jumped into the conversation at that point. "Tailor made for you, Brother. Pick a good spot to eagle for us. Say when and where."

"Affirm," responded Loudelk's cool whisper.

"Somebody better get on me then," Zitka advised. "This old bomb may not hang together much longer."

"Coming up," Bolan reported. He power shifted the little car into a smooth leap forward, the tach climbing steadily toward the max line.

The voices of Harrington and Washington took over then, signaling the Horse's arrival on the Riverside cut-off. Bolan picked up the radio and said, "Welcome aboard. Close on me with all speed."

"Gotcha," Harrington replied.

"Have you been following the play?"

" 'Firmative. Understand, north at the buttes wye."

"You know this area, Guns?"

"Like my own little sandbox."

"What's up in those buttes?"

"Not much. A few citrus farms. Couple of ranches."

"Okay. Continue closing. Tracker, I've got you in sight now. What the hell happened to Brother?"

"Dunno. Saw a cloud of dust in my rear view a minute ago. Think he took a dirt road."

"Tracker Two, report," Bolan commanded. "Bloodbrother!"

An agonizing silence followed. Bolan was now deep into the buttes and casting anxious glances onto the terrain to either side of him. The Corvette hurtled on, maintaining the visual track on Zitka. Presently Loudelk's smooth baritone boomed in loud and clear: "Eagle is on station. Situation magnificent. Instructions."

"Do you have quarry in sight?" Bolan snapped.

"Affirm, and half the country from L.A. to Riverside."

"Report terrain conclusions!"

"Dirt road, leading east, about . . . three miles beyond present position of quarry. Greenery at end of road—trees, I guess. No other exits visible."

"Break off ground track!" Bolan immediately commanded. "I want a wilco."

"Wilco, and just in time," Zitka responded. "I'm heating up."

Bolan slowed his vehicle. "Where are you from my present position, Eagle?" he asked.

"You passed me 'bout a minute ago."

"Good. Maintain eagle watch and report developments. Backboard, you and Horse pour on the coals, get up here as quick as you can."

"Roger."

Zitka had pulled the Mercury onto the shoulder of the road and was standing beside it. Bolan stopped and picked him up, then resumed a leisurely advance. He thumbed on the transmitter and said, "Backboard, one of you transfer to the wagon. It's on the side track just ahead of you."

"Roger," Washington replied. "I'll take it."

"Horse, keep closing until further instructions."

"Roger."

"You cooled it right, Maestro," Loudelk came in. "They just pulled onto the dirt road and stopped. Like they're waiting."

Bolan grinned and allowed the Corvette to begin coasting to a halt. "Good show," he told Loudelk. "Maintain watch." He swiveled about and looked behind him. "I can see your smoke, Horse. Keep rolling. Quarry has gone to ground about three minutes ahead. Proceed on beyond them, then come about at first convenient spot and hold. Backboard, fall back to the wye with both vehicles and look innocent. Report all passings onto this road."

"Gotcha."

"Backboard, roger."

"Now," Bolan said to Zitka, "we will separate the foxes from the hounds."

Emilio Giordano was in a very nasty mood. Nothing could possibly be right at the ranch on such a day. He fired two of the freight handlers who were engaged in a playful slap fight at the loading dock; then he chewed on the ranch manager for not having an up-to-the-minute inventory of the warehouse. A few minutes later he physically attacked the nervous young man with the briefcase and told the world at large, in loud and certain terms, what he was going to do to Bruno "when and if he ever finds his way here!"

Bruno and the other four occupants of the rear-guard Continental did show up about thirty minutes after Giordano's arrival. The grillwork of the expenisve automobile was misshapen here and there, and the glass was missing from the head-lamps.

"We got into an accident," Bruno reported, his voice muted in the face of his employer's towering rage.

"*We got into an accident,*" Giordano mimicked in a mealy-mouthed twang. "You son of a bitch you! I oughta kill you! I oughta *kill* you!"

"Christ's sake, 'Milio, it could happen to anybody," Bruno protested.

"It don't not supposed to happen to *you!*" Giordano screamed in tongue-twisting rage. "What if those bastards'd jumped me? Huh? Huh? Where was Bruno when those bastards jumped 'Milio, eh? I oughta . . ." He stepped forward and delivered a stinging slap to Bruno's face, then hit him with the other hand.

The bodyguard stoically accepted the indignities, though paling somewhat with suppressed anger. "I couldn't help it," he muttered. "We got into a tangle on the freeway, and we got hooked onto a cop's rear bumper."

"A *cop*? A *cop*?"

"Yeh. That's why we were delayed so long. Had to show our licenses for the hardware; then they had to make out this full report on the accident, and . . . well, the cops were pretty damn pissed off, too. I thought for a minute there—"

"Spare me," Giordano groaned. "Spare me the dumbhead details. Get inna car. Get inna goddamn car! We're goin' back. We'll start all over again." He summoned the briefcase bearer with a wave of his hand, then shoved him roughly toward the Rolls.

The ranch manager was standing nearby, a strained expression on his face. "Lookit this," Giordano fumed, turning to the manager. "I go to all this planning, I even bring my shakin' bookkeeper with twenty-five thou just to make the armed guard look legit for the cops, we come all the way out here—and for what? For what? For Bruno the Brilliant to lock bumpers with a cop car? Huh? Is that what it was all for?" His rage was quickly wearing itself out. "How much is in the exchange box?" he asked the manager.

"Seventy thou," the manager replied. "You want to pick it up?"

Giordano nodded. "With my luck today, sergeant dumbhead will wander in here lost, an hour after I leave, and decide to knock the joint over." He swiveled about and called Bruno. "Hey, Brains. Go get the box."

Bruno got out of the car and followed the manager into the office. Giordano called after him, "Try'n carry it to the car without having an accident, eh?"

Minutes later, the small caravan was headed back along the dirt road, the white Rolls sandwiched between the two black Continentals, and this time with Bruno's vehicle leading. The bookkeeper sat quietly alongside Giordano, the

68

briefcase on his lap, a small metal box between his feet.

"Hey, kid, I'm sorry I lost my temper, eh?" Giordano said quietly.

"Sure, Mr. Giordano. I understand."

"Just one of those damn days, I guess," Giordano muttered. "Guess it couldn't get much worse, eh?"

"I guess not, sir."

But it did, very shortly.

"Motorcade on the trail," Loudelk reported calmly.

"Roger," Bolan replied. "Anything to our rear?"

"Negative," Loudelk said, from his high observation point. "All clear."

"Last thing through the wye was the dented Detroit black," Washington reported.

"Roger. You set, Horse?"

"Horse is set," Harrington's voice reported.

"Then roll it."

The whine of a motor-driven winch broke the stillness. A big boulder at the side of the roadway began to dance with vibration, then tilted and rolled abruptly onto the roadway. The winch was silenced. Zitka and Andromede ran out to the boulder, freed a network of cables, and dragged them into the shadow of a high butte.

The death squad could not have found a better location for an ambush. They were about midway between the blacktop county road and the citrus grove, at a point where the private dirt road curved abruptly to thread between two high-ridged rock formations. The roadblock was dropped directly into the eye of this needle, halfway through and just beyond a ninety-degree curve. The jeep had been unloaded from the horse and was angled into the shadow of the butte just beyond the roadblock, with its big fifty caliber commanding the situation there. Andromede was manning the fifty.

Zitka had the left flank, Bolan the right, both with light automatic weapons and with good cover on high ground that allowed a good triangulation of firepower.

Gunsmoke Harrington was at the front end of the needle, ahead of the roadblock. His six-guns were strapped low, and a light automatic was slung at his chest. He would plug any attempted retreat.

"Coming up on one mile," Loudelk reported.

Bolan thumbed the transmitter and snapped, "Roger." Then, "Backboard, start your move. Hold at the junction of the dirt road."

He received acknowledgements from Blancanales and Washington, then tossed the radio aside and waited.

They came on fast, as if they knew the road was their very own, the dust from the lead vehicles all but obscuring the third car in the file. Bruno swung the big Continental expertly into the curve, as he had done so many times before, and then was frantically grabbing for more brake pedal than he would ever find. Bolan could see electrified alarm replace the dreamy smile on the handsome face; he could see Bruno's body stiffening and the tightened fingers clawing at the steering wheel.

It was a long microsecond. Then the Continental was trying to climb the barricade and failing to do so as three tons of hurtling metal met sixteen tons of unmoving rock. The grinding crash sent a bodyless head arcing through the shattered windshield, to bounce along the quickly shriveling hood. The passenger compartment continued moving briefly after the forward part had come to rest, telescoping into the flattened engine compartment—and then the armored Rolls smashed into the rear, brakes screaming and horn blaring inanely. Almost instantly the third crash came as the rear Continental plowed into the Rolls.

To this bedlam was suddenly added the staccato chopping of the big fifty as Andromede began spraying the wreckage with steel-jacketed projectiles. A man staggered out of the third car, firing blindly into the rock walls with a pistol. A higher-pitched chatter responded immediately from both sides of the trap, and the man was flung backward, and down, and dead.

Incredibly, fire was being returned from the Rolls, and the heavy vehicle was rocking forward and backward, the powerful engine straining mightily as the driver fought to extricate the armored car from the jamming smashup.

"It's a tank, all right," Bolan grunted to himself, noting the battering-ram writhing of the Rolls. He snatched up his radio and barked into it, "Gunsmoke! Bring up the big stick!"

All three members of the fire team were now concentrating their assault on the Rolls, Andromede from almost point-blank range. Still it snorted and struggled like an enraged bull elephant caught in a bog, and still a sporadic return fire issued from it. Then Bolan caught a glimpse of Harrington sprinting around the curve, a long tubelike object hefted onto his shoulder. He watched him approach to within 100 feet of the Rolls, then drop to one knee and sight in the bazooka. An instant later the familiar whoosh, fire, and smoke of the armor-piercing rocket was introduced to the Battle at the Buttes, the enraged bull elephant was enveloped in a deafening explosion, and its struggles immediately ceased.

"Awright, awright!" a voice screamed out a moment later. A thickset man staggered out of the smoke and into the open.

Bolan sprang atop the rock that had served as his cover and called down, "Time to pay the tab, Giordano."

"Dumbhead!" the Maffiano screamed. His arm jerked up, and the .38 reported three times. The third report, however, was no more than the spasmodic reflex of a quickly dying muscle. Bolan had fired from the hip in one rapid burst that split the rackateer's body from groin to skull, and Il Fortunato was dead on his feet.

All in all, the battle had lasted less than two minutes. Zitka took a blackened briefcase and a metal box from the passenger compartment of the Rolls. The heavy weapons and the spoils were tossed into the jeep. Andromede jumped behind the wheel and sped off toward the rear of the needle.

Zitka told Bolan, "There's a guy still alive back there. In the tank."

Bolan sent Zitka and Harrington on to the vehicles and went to investigate Zitka's report. He found a frightened young man cringing on the smoldering rear floor of the still-smoking Rolls, tightly gripping a bleeding shoulder.

"I-I'm just his bookkeeper," the casualty moaned.

Bolan holstered his .45, reached into his first-aid pouch and tossed a sterile compress onto the seat. "Know nothing, see nothing, say nothing," Bolan growled. "That way you may live awhile."

The bookkeeper jerked his head in a vigorous assent. Bolan spun away and ran to rejoin the others. The jeep was already inside the van, and Harrington was pacing nervously alongside the retractable ramps. "Anything else for the horse?" he yelled, as soon as he noted Bolan's approach.

"Not yet," Bolan replied. "Pick up the wagon

down at the blacktop. Then head for home—the long way."

"Gotcha." Harrington was already rolling the ramps into the van. Andromede hastened to assist him. Bolan and Zitka sprinted to the Corvette.

Zitka was reaching for the radio as Bolan spun the sportster around. "How do you say, Eagle?" he demanded into the transmitter.

"Clean, man, clean," Loudelk's drawl came back. "And I missed all the fun."

"Okay, split," Zitka told him.

"Affirm, I am splitting."

Bolan glanced at Zitka and said, "Tell Deadeye about the wagon."

Zitka nodded and again spoke into the radio. "The wagon goes in the horse," he said. "Backboard regroup in the Mustang and head for the stable."

"Roger," responded a strained voice. "Is anything wrong with Maestro?"

"Naw, I'm just riding shotgun and radio for him. God, it went great, great, and I think we got another boodle."

"I see your dust," Washington reported. "Glad it went good. Next time I want up front."

Bolan grinned and reached for the radio. He depressed the transmitter button and said, "Good show, group, all of you, but play it cool now until we're home clean. Radio silence, beginning right now, except for emergencies. Read?"

"Read," replied Deadeye Washington.

"Gotcha," said Harrington.

"Affirm," reported Bloodbrother Loudelk.

"Wilco," Blancanales responded.

Chapter Seven

FACE TO FACE

Captain Braddock was perturbed. Worse than that, he was beginning to feel a bit unsure of himself. He turned away from the large map on the wall of his office and faced his Hardcase-detail leaders. The two lieutenants and four sergeants who stared back at him had been carefully selected for this project. Each was an outstanding officer with an unblemished record of police efficiency.

"All right," Braddock said quietly, "what went wrong?"

Lieutenant Andy Foster cleared his throat and ran a hand through his hair. He and Braddock had been friends since police-academy days. "We underestimated the guy," he flatly declared.

"He did it so smoothly, I didn't even realize I'd been sucked in," spoke up a young sergeant, Carl Lyons. "Not until I started putting the pieces together."

"There was a confusion factor," Foster explained, as though to soften Lyon's admission. "First off, Giordano comes out in *two* vehicles. Somewhere along the line, God knows where, he added a third. Carl had no way of identifying the players. Cars were jumping into that procession all the way down to the freeway. It was pretty obvious that Giordano was trying to provoke a fight, and we simply had no way of determining which of those vehicles were Giordano's, which were Bolan's if any, and which were just unwitting participants. I ordered Carl to simply stay on Giordano's tail and report developments."

"I kept looking for a sudden strike," Lyons admitted. "I guess I really wasn't thinking in terms of a Bolan tail. I was just trying to hang in there on Giordano. We hit the freeway, and I tried to tighten it up some. Then, zot!—I'm trapped into the cloverleaf of the interchange with another car hung on my rear bumper."

"And you immediately reported your trouble?" Braddock inquired.

"Sure. I was in contact with Lieutenant Foster the whole time."

"I realized we'd lost Giordano," Foster said. "It was 3:30 the peak period was beginning, and the freeways were beginning to pack. We're spread too thin, Tim. If we'd had three times our capability, we still couldn't have covered all possibilities—not short of a general alert. I had to cover the Golden State, the San Bernardino, the Santa Ana, and I couldn't even positively write off the harbor."

"Yeah," Braddock grunted. His guts were faintly churning.

"And remember, we had no way of knowing that Bolan was even interested in Giordano at that particular time. If I'd punched the panic button and sent all the Hardcase vehicles scurrying after Giordano, that would have left the rest of the possibilities free and clear for Bolan to tap. You said he was a brilliant tactician. I had to assume that—"

"Of course, Andy," Braddock interrupted. "You played it right. No criticism there."

"I played it *safe*, not right," Foster muttered. "I alerted the neighboring communities and asked them to put out a soft watch for the Giordano vehicles, and then I stewed and chewed my nails and waited for a contact report."

The other lieutenant present, Charlie Rickert, joined the discussion at that point. The man unofficially referred to as "the twenty-four-hour cop" said, "The biggest goof was our failure to tail Bruno Scarelli. I think that was dumb. He was our one sure lead to Giordano's destination."

Carl Lyons flushed a deep scarlet. "I had to make a decision, and I made it," he said. "I detained Scarelli as long as I could, without tipping our hand. Couldn't tail him myself, not with that rear fender buckled in on the wheel. When one of those big cars tap your butt, you damn well know you've been tapped." He rubbed the back of his neck and scowled at Rickert.

"I sent a car to cover Scarelli," Foster reported, tight lipped. "Got there about thirty seconds late and lost him right back at that same damn interchange."

"I still think—"

Rickert's knife-twisting rejoiner was interrupted by the appearance of a uniformed officer in the doorway. "Got that report from the Riverside lab, Captain," he announced.

"Let's hear it," Braddock clipped.

"It was an armor-piercing projectile, all right. Probably fired from a bazooka. Slammed into the Rolls just forward of the doorpost, angling in from the rear. Instant death for the two men in front. The other scars were made by steel-jacketed slugs from a fifty-caliber machine gun. Each of the vehicles was pretty thoroughly worked over by that fifty."

"Thanks, Art," Braddock replied. The uniformed officer smiled and went away, shaking his head. "Full-scale warfare," Braddock growled.

"And the neatest ambush I've ever . . ." Foster commented, his voice trailing off into quiet speculation.

Rickert reached into his pocket, withdrew a long metallic object, and tossed it onto Braddock's desk. "There was a small mountain of these fifty-caliber

76

casings in the rocks over against the butte," he said.

Braddock picked up the casing and absently turned it end over end in his big hand. "They had that jeep out there, that's certain," he concluded. "Now somebody tell me how they can run around in an armed jeep without arousing curiosity? Where are they getting this heavy stuff—the bazooka and all that crap? How the hell did they move that heavy boulder onto the road? How the hell . . . ?"

Lieutenant Rickert sighed heavily and produced a small notebook from his jacket pocket. "I may have some answers," he said. "I spent the past three hours sifting through the various reports, and . . . well, just listen. From the Bel Air investigation: The jeep was last seen proceeding north on Skylane Drive. Yet two witnesses at the next intersection, swear that no jeep came past them. Aside from the police and fire-department vehicles, the only moving thing reported through that intersection, in that time period, was a large diesel semitrailer van. The witness paid it very little attention, and couldn't recall any identifying decals, or even the color." Rickert glanced at Sergeant Lyons. "Next I quote from Carl's report: '. . . and I was forced to follow a slow-moving semitrailer into the cloverleaf.'" Rickert smiled wryly. "You did not specify, Carl. This wouldn't have been a van-type trailer, would it?"

Lyons silently nodded his head, staring speculatively into the lieutenant's eyes.

"Uh-huh. The plot thickens. Now—from the statement by Giordano's accountant, the sole survivor of the ambush: 'Mr. Giordano thought we were being followed on the way out there, and we even waited at the back road to let them catch up; he was trying to lure them into a trap. But the only thing that came along was a big diesel truck. It was a blue-and-white moving van, I believe." Rickert angled a glance at the captain. "It, uh, could be entirely coincidental. Then, again, there could be an answer in there."

A fire had been lighted in Braddock's eyes. "The clever bastard," he murmured.

"You think it's too strong for coincidence?" Foster asked.

"I'm not leaving anything to coincidence!" Braddock snapped. "Not when Bolan's hand is in it." He whirled around to his desk and shuffled through a pile of papers, came up with one, and hastily skimmed down the typewritten lines. "Here it is," he announced. "This is the transcript of the interrogation of Gerald Young, the accountant. He was questioned as to why Giordano had felt they were being tailed. He says: 'Well, I thought so myself. There were these same two cars that kept showing up behind us. One was a blue Ford sedan, late model, and the other was an older station wagon, a big one. Maybe a Buick or a Mercury.'" Braddock's eyes swung to Carl Lyons. "Ring any bells, Sergeant?"

The young officer's eyes were haunted pools of revelation. "The blue Ford joined the procession at Lani Way," he growled. "The wagon joined up at the arterial, just behind me. We hit the on ramp in that order—the big Continental, the Rolls, the Ford, me, the station wagon. Then everything got scrambled up when we moved into the freeway traffic. I was concentrating on the Rolls."

"They had you spotted all the way!" Rickert howled. "Hell, boy, they suckered you and packaged you off neat and clean."

"How the hell was I supposed to keep on Giordano and every other damn car on the freeway at the same time? I never gave a passing thought to those other cars—and certainly not to a *semi*. Who would?"

"Carl is right," Braddock muttered. "Anyone would have jerked up damn quick, though, if a military jeep with a wicked-looking machine gun on the rear deck had joined the parade. That clever bastard. That's how he's doing it. He's using a Trojan horse. He could pack a small armored unit in that van."

"I wouldn't be surprised if the sonofabitch had a *tank* in there," Foster declared.

Braddock ignored the remark. "Carl—think carefully now. Which vehicle actually sprung the trap on you? The Ford or the wagon?"

"Neither one," Lyons replied immediately. "I've been trying to . . . I was so pissed off, I . . . Wait, now. I was wondering why he was going so slow, and it . . . Sure! It was a sports car, a red sports car!"

"What make?"

"Damn, I . . . Out-of-state tags. I remember, now, I was thinking, if you can't drive on our freeways, even with a roadrunner like that one, then keep the hell off. Then I started around him, and that was all she wrote."

"The timing for that little trick must have been fantastic," Foster observed. "And it couldn't have been just a spontaneous thing. They had to have radios in those cars."

"Goddammit!" Braddock said softly.

"That adds an entire new dimension to this thing," Rickert put in.

"Why not?" Braddock muttered. "Why shouldn't he think of radios? They're as much a military tool as a gun. And hell, you can practically buy them in dime stores nowadays." He paused, then added thoughtfully, "We have to completely revamp our strategy. Let's see if we can't find a way to inter-

79

cept their radio signals. Andy, I'm making that your responsibility. Electronic intelligence gathering is a sophisticated science, so you'll have to dig up some expert assistance. Try the FCC—hell, try the army and the navy, and the CIA, if necessary—but let's get something working on this angle."

"This is a smoothly oiled machine we're going against. These guys are going to make us look like monkeys unless we . . ." He left the statement dangling and turned worried eyes to twenty-four-hour Rickert. "Well, Chuck, it looks like you've called the play on this thing. Let's learn all we can about these vehicles they're using. Get the information to all units as quickly as possible. Shake as many people as possible onto this semitrailer. A thing like that must be hard to conceal if it isn't in motion or parked in a terminal. Check out every possible lead, anything and everything unusual regarding the use or the location of a van-type semi. Follow up on the weapons angle, Carl. You just don't pick up bazookas and machine guns at the neighborhood hardware store. Look into recent purchases of sophisticated radio equipment. I want an around-the-clock effort. I want every—"

"It's nearly midnight, Tim," Foster reminded the captain. "Some of our people have logged fourteen straight hours already."

"I'm getting you some more poeple," Braddock assured him. "I want this thing covered. I want it—"

He was interrupted again by the same uniformed officer charging through the doorway. "They're at it again!" he reported breathlessly. "Just hit Tri-Coast Records in Burbank!"

"A recording company?" Braddock seemed stunned. "What makes you think it's Bolan? I don't get the—"

"I don't know about that," the officer said. "It's at the distribution warehouse out on Studio Way. They just said some guys are running around out there throwing firebombs and shooting up the place with choppers. Sounds like a Hardcase to me!"

Braddock was already out the door, the officer on his heels, the group of lawmen following close behind and spilling into the special Hardcase control room. Braddock spun on them and barked, "Get going! I'll feed you via radio!"

The detail leaders about-faced and jogged into the corridor, heading for the garage. Braddock, at the control console, depressed a button and bawled, "Dispatch. Hardcase alert, all available units. Code 7-10 and double it! Burbank Studio City, Santa Monica, Glendale, converge on Alpha that is Alpha Four, and stand by further."

He did not wait for an acknowledgement from the central dispatcher but flipped another switch, picked up a pedestal-type microphone, and began hurling instructions into the Hardcase special network.

Sergeant Carl Lyons, jogging down the long tunnel toward the garage at the side of Lieutenant Foster, said, "Is this guy for real? Three hits in one day! He moves fast!"

Foster was getting winded. "Makes you wonder why we haven't won the war in Vietnam, doesn't it?" he panted. "And I'm getting the feeling that we're losing this one."

"We'll get 'im!" Lyons snapped. "I just want to meet the guy face to face, that's all."

"Myself, I think we oughta call in artillery and air support. This's no job for cops. That bastard might have a Sherman tank out there. He might have a goddamn B-52, and I wouldn't be a damn bit surprised."

Lyons chuckled and split away. They had reached the garage. He sprinted to his car, which his waiting partner already had in motion. Lyons hoped they would catch Bolan in the net this time. He wanted to meet the clever bastard face to face. He wanted to thank him for making a total idiot out of the quote most promising young detective sergeant on the force, unquote. He wanted to thank him with a bullet up each nostril.

"Okay, break off!" Bolan yelled into his radio. The warehouse was blazing furiously, great mushrooms of roaring flames boiling high overhead and turning night into day for a hundred yards in all directions, intense heat generating into an inpenetrable barrier surrounding the long structure.

"Yea, man!" Chopper Fontenelli sang back. "Listen to it sizzle. Whatta they make these records out of, anyway?"

Bolan was jumping for his vehicle, parked along the fence at the back of the lot. He jumped inside, clipped the radio to a fixture above the dash, and fishtailed along the graveled back lot in a full-power swoop toward the warehouse office at the far corner. There he collected Boom-Boom Hoffower, who had been standing a casual guard over a small collection of warehouse employees, evacuated just prior to the incendiary attack. Hoffower swung the door open and nonchalantly slid into the seat alongside Bolan.

"And I forgot to bring the marshmallows," he sighed.

Bolan grunted into the gears and sent the little speedster whining along the macadam drive. They flashed through the open gateway and skidded into the street, then straightened in a full-throttle roar toward the distant line of hills. They were free and clear. Bolan tensed over the wheel and poked a finger at the transmitter button. "Chopper! Where away?"

There was no response to the query. Bolan's foot held steady on the accelerator. Hoffower fidgeted, then reached for the radio. Just as his hand closed on it, Fontenelli's voice came through in a breathless wail. "Sarge! Fuzz all over the place!"

Bolan muttered something under his breath. His hand and foot moved in concert, the hand toward the radio, the foot heavy on the brake. The Corvette was still sliding to a squealing halt when he barked into the radio, "Situation, Chopper!"

Fontenelli's excited voice flashed back immediately. "My gas tank blew! Vehicle's burning! I'm hurt. Fuzz crawling heavy. Gate blocked. I'm sewed in!"

The Corvette was spinning into a U-turn across the country road, Bolan twirling the wheel with one hand and operating the radio with the other. "Get to the northwest corner of the fence and lay low. I'm coming after you."

"Make it damn quick."

"Cool it! Just cool it and watch for me! We'll get you out, Chopper!"

Carl Lyons could see the flames leaping high above the valley floor. The wail of sirens and the heavy gut-rumble of fire trucks were lacing the night and adding to the unreality of the scene. His driver tromped the accelerator pedal and leaned into the curving approach to the warehouse area just as the radio crackled and Captain Braddock's crisp tones joined them. "Hardcase units 1, 3, 5, and 7, attention—Hardcase alert—Zone immediate! Divert and stand by further."

"Christ, they're hitting in Hollywood, too," Officer Evers commented, glancing at Lyons. His foot faltered on the accelerator.

"Forget it, we're on this one now!" Lyons snapped. They were threading between a line of parked patrol cars. Uniformed officers in white helmets and carrying riot guns could be seen moving cautiously on from in the compound. A fire captain was vigorously waving Lyon's vehicle through, to clear the drive. Firemen were darting about in the intense heat, dragging hoses and other paraphernalia.

Braddock's voice had returned to the air. ". . . screen across all Zone 2 intersections between King Five and King Nine. Close and apprehend. Unit 3, acknowledge."

Evers stared morosely at Lyons. "Are you going to acknowledge?" he asked tightly.

The sergeant was leaving the vehicle. He leaned tensely back through the doorway and said, "You acknowledge, if you want to. Tell him we're already here and I'm out of the vehicle."

"I better acknowledge," Evers replied, reaching for the mike. Lyons was even then out of earshot, moving swiftly into the confusion.

George Zitka was pounding along a narrow alleyway, a canvas bag suspended from his shoulder. Deadeye Washington loped along at his heels, the long legs moving in an effortless stride, an automatic weapon riding across his chest, a smaller bag dangling from a huge hand. They angled across a deserted parking lot, passing to the rear of a taco house, and spurted across Vine Street. A Ford sedan eased around a corner, moving slowly. They ran alongside the Ford for a short distance, passing weapons and other burdens through the open windows; then the doors opened, and Zitka

84

and Washington flung themselves inside, the car already picking up speed.

Gunsmoke Harrington, behind the wheel, asked anxiously, "How'd it go?"

Washington chuckled and said, "Scared the pee out of bigshot Varone. He insisted we take the money—just plain insisted. We obliged him."

Zitka was panting with exertion. "We caught 'im throwin' one into some hot little blonde."

"Yeah?" Harrington swiveled his head about in a long stare at Zitka, then almost reluctantly returned his attention to the road. He swung into a sidestreet and gunned along in second gear to the next intersection and swerved into the approach to the Hollywood Freeway. "How come I miss all the fun?" he groused.

"Hell, *he* was having the fun, *we* wasn't," Washington replied. "Anyway, she seemed almost glad to see us. He was probably making her put out to get herself on a record. I hear these guys do that."

A police car, beacon flashing angrily, tore past them in the opposite direction. "Wonder where he's going?" Harrington asked, grinning.

"I bet he's headed for that recording studio," Zitka said. He flashed an amused glance toward Washington. "You know—that place back there where we heard all the commotion?"

Deadeye Washington was all smiles. "Sounded to me like somebody was just tearin' hell out of all that expensive equipment. Wonder who'd want to do a thing like that?"

The Ford was on the freeway ramp and angling for a shot into the traffic. Harrington stiffened momentarily, his eyes following a speeding vehicle that had just zipped past them. "There goes Bloodbrother," he announced. "Looks like our timing was perfect." Harrington found his spot and moved the

Ford smoothly into the flow of traffic. "Wonder how the sarge is doing with his strike."

"Don't you worry none about that man," Washington said softly. "He knows where it is, man, and what it is and how it is. Don't you worry none about that soul."

Sweat was running down Carl Lyons's arms and dripping from the tips of his fingers. He could not have said, moments earlier, whether it had been the incredible heat or some stubborn cop's instinct that had driven him to this corner of the yard, but the muffled explosion along the fence corner suddenly assured him that fate had placed him there, whatever the form of persuasion. He sensed, more than saw, the movement of the tall grass near the fence. His weapon was in his hand before he even realized it, and he was in a weirdly frozen eyeball-to-eyeball encounter with a grinning ape and a light machine gun. The man was clad in army fatigues and a dark beret, with crossed, solid-state two-way radio was strapped to his shoulder. He was kneeling on one knee and grinning up at Lyons over the sights of the very efficient-looking automatic weapon.

"Drop it," Lyons instinctively commanded.

"Huh-uh," the other man said, still grinning.

The noise and confusion a bare hundred yards distant seemed entirely remote and part of an entirely different reality, the dancing firelight adding to the weirdness of the scene.

"This is no Mexican standoff, Bolan," Lyons said, his voice slightly quivering in the contained excitement. "I'm police officer, and I'm ordering you to drop your weapon."

"I'm not Bolan. Go ahead and shoot. You'll reach hell one sure step ahead of me."

Lyons's blood ran cold as another voice joined

the conversation. It was cool and deliberate, and it was saying, "Thumb off, Chopper, and walk away." A tall man was standing on the outide of the chain link fence. Lyons suddenly understood the explosion that had focused his attention to the spot. The center post was half-concealed in a cloud of black smoke; it was twisted grotesquely, and torn strands of the chain link were clinging to it. One section of the fence was curling back toward the next supporting post. They had blown the fence.

The tall man with the cold voice was holding an army .45 at arm's length, and he was pointing the gun at the grinning ape.

"I ain't used to walkin' away, Sarge," the ape snarled.

"It's either walk or be carried, Chopper," the cool voice advised.

Lyons experienced a vague sense of mental confusion. The big guy was taking *his* part. "Just a minute," Lyons said thickly. "No one is walking away."

"Start walking, Chopper," the tall man commanded sternly, ignoring Lyons's protest completely.

The ape was still grinning but without humor. A growl rattled in his throat; then he got slowly to his feet, his eyes remaining hard and unflickering on the lawman.

Lyons felt dazed. His ears roared. The .38 police special seemed to be hanging out there in front of him of its own volition; yet he was very strongly aware of the slowly tightening pressure of his finger upon the trigger. The ape took a slow backward step, then another; carefully placing his feet on the uneven ground. Lyons angled his gaze toward the tall man. "You're Bolan," he said.

The man nodded curtly. "No fight with you, Officer," he said lightly.

"Since when?" Lyons asked. He did not recognize the sound of his own voice.

Bolan was moving softly toward the ape now, getting between the slowly retreating figure and Lyons. "Never have," he intoned soberly. "You're right, and I'm right." His eyes flicked toward the burning warehouse. "There's the wrong ones. There's my fight."

The ape was fading fast now. Lyons wondered vaguely why he was just standing there. Bolan's .45 was now moving slowly down and in. He eased it into the flap of the holster. "Now I'm walking," he said softly.

Lyons shoved his pistol to full arm-extension toward the tall, black-clad figure. "You're under arrest, Bolan," he snapped.

"I'm walking," Bolan repeated. He spun on his heel and faded silently into the darkness.

Lyons stared unbelievingly at the spot where The Executioner had stood. He lowered his revolver and poked it angrily into the holster. The sound of running feet advanced from the confused din at his back, and a moment later two uniformed officers drew up alongside him.

"I *thought* that explosion came from back here," one of the officers exclaimed. He knelt down and laid a hand on the section of fallen fence, then hastily jerked it away. "Damn, it's still hot. You see anything, sir?"

"Must have been a timed explosive," Lyons muttered. "Damn thing practically blew up in my face."

"You didn't see anything, eh?"

"No." Lyons gazed out into the darkness beyond the fence. So—he'd met the clever bastard face to face. And let him simply walk away. "No, I didn't see anything," he said calmly.

Chapter Eight

THE BORNING DEAD

It was just a few minutes before 3:00 A.M., and Zeno Varone knew that there was no sleep in the cards for him this night. He had been pacing back and forth across his sumptuous office for fully ten minutes, ever since the investigating police cleared out, his anger building into a great weighted ball right in the middle of his throat, and he knew that ball would not dissolve until he could spray it back out onto the lunatics who had placed it there. He halted in midstride, legs spread far apart, and brought a fist crashing onto the back rest of a leathered chair.

"How the *hell* did they get onto me?" he yelled. "How did they know?" He whirled about and jabbed a stiff index finger toward the man who calmly perched on the corner of his desk. "You find out! You hear me? That's what you're getting paid for!"

The other man casually took a drag from his cigarette and blew the smoke toward the ceiling. "Don't remind me of my sins, Varone," he replied lightly. "Don't get too shook up, either. We'll have this guy on ice soon enough."

"Soon *enough*?" Varone was all but frothing at the mouth. "I'm telling you, *right now* is not soon enough. Those sonsabitches walked out of here with twenty grand—yeah, yeah, not like I told your pals—twenty grand in cool cash that wasn't even mine. That was *family* money. Not to mention, hell, not to mention what they did downstairs. I don't even know if my insurance will pay off on this stuff. They'll probably call it an act of war or something. Do you realize? I'm out of business. I'm out of business until I can get all that stuff replaced."

The other man nodded his head soberly and leaned across the desk to crush out his cigarette. "I wonder how your distributor, Strecchio, is taking his loss?"

"Hell, he don't have a nickel of his own in Tri-Coast. It's all organization money, every nickel of it. What's he got to cry about? The discs were *mine*, not his."

The man grunted, then eased onto the floor and stepped over a window, thrust his hands into his pockets, and gazed down onto the street. "You've overlooked the most important item," he said.

"*What* have I overlooked?"

"Well, we'd managed to keep your name clean all this time. You're not in *our* files, you're not on the Attorney General's list—but somehow you got yourself onto Bolan's list. So now you're on everybody's list and in everybody's files. Bolan exposed you, Varone. He blew the whistle on you."

"That son of a *bitch!*"

"Yeah. You hadn't thought of that, eh?"

"Listen! You gotta do your job! You hear? We ain't been giving you two grand a month to just—"

"Cut it!" the man demanded, his voice deepening in anger. "Don't ever tell me what my job is, Zeno. My job is what I make it. And don't ever tell me what you give me. And for God's sake, don't fall apart. Now—we know a lot about the guy already. We know how he operates, we have a line on some of his vehicles, and pretty soon—pretty soon—we'll have this Bolan on ice. Don't sweat it."

"I'm calling in the family."

"That would be your very worse mistake! Why do you think they left you living, Zeno? Don't you see this is what they want you to do?"

"Don't tell *me*. Your cops—they're pretty hot stuff, eh? They run a tight city, eh?" Varone began laughing in an almost hysterical outburst. He went over to the liquor cabinet, mixed whiskey and water in a careless blend, and gulped half of it down. The other man was glaring at him with an angry frown. Varone wiped his lips with the back of his hand and said, "That's the same thing I told 'Milio, you know. Well, where's poor 'Milio now? Huh? Let me tell you something, Mr. Hot Stuff. Your cops are dead on their ass. Know that? They're from nowhere. I'm going to bring some *real* class into this problem. I'm not going to sit back and let this guy dance lightly around, stealing and killing, slapping me on the ass, terrorizing my broads, tearing up my property. I'm not going to do that. You're outta your mind if you think I am."

"You're making the same panicky mistake 'Milio made," the visitor pointed out. "You're deciding to fight the guy on his terms."

"No, no—not on *his* terms; *my* terms, Charlié. We fight on the *same* terms, see—only I got a hell of a lot more experience. *And* a lot more class."

"Class will tell, won't it? You know, Zeno, at this moment you are looking and thinking and talking just exactly like the small-time hood you really are."

"Get outta here, you bastard you!" Varone snarled. His hand tightened around the glass, the knuckles whitening with tension.

"You're sure that's what you want?"

"I'm sure."

"All right, gladly," replied the other in a pleasant voice, and Charlie Rickert, full-time cop and part-time Maffiano, went quietly to the door and got out of there.

"Hey, I'm ready for some R and R," Andromede

announced. He dropped to the floor in front of the couch and flaked out, face down, his forehead resting on an unflung arm.

"He got rich in one day and he's bitching," Fontenelli observed, winking at Blancanales.

"But oh, my nerves," Andromede said in a muffled voice.

Blancanales was delicately applying a burn ointment to a reddened area of Fontenelli's shoulder. "Don't find many men with hair on their *shoulders*," he muttered, then added, "It's not a bad burn, Chopper. Could a been a lot worse, considering."

Fontenelli merely grunted.

"Hell, it's three o'clock," Andromede announced. "Let's get some sacktime."

"We're gonna hit 'em, and hit 'em, and keep on hittin' 'em," Fontenelli declared, in a fair imitation of Bolan's voice, "until Flower Child starts crying for some sacktime."

"Up your butt, brother," Andromede replied quietly.

Bolan entered from the kitchen, carrying a sandwich and coffee. "How's the shoulder look, Politician?" he asked.

"More pain than damage," Blancanales assured him.

"But not enough pain to straighten his brain," Andromede added. He rose to a kneeling position and rocked back on his haunches, staring expectantly at Bolan.

Bolan was positioning a TV tray in front of a chair. He sat down, pulled the tray closer, and sampled the coffee. "We got lucky," he said simply.

Fontenelli flexed his massive shoulders and directed a veiled gaze at Bolan. "The sarge pulled leather on me tonight," he announced casually.

Deadeye Washington, seated in a large recliner

across the room, chuckled and said, "And you're able to talk about it? I guess you did get lucky, then."

"Yeah." Fontenelli was still staring at Bolan. "I think everybody oughta know—he also pulled me outta one hell of a bad spot. He was free and clear, and he came back to get me out. I'll never forget that, Sarge."

Bolan swallowed a chunk of sandwich and nodded his head. "I'd like to think you'd do the same for me, Chopper."

A grin slowly spread across Fontenelli's dark face. "Sorry I got out of line. It won't happen again."

Bolan winked at him, then turned his attention to Gadgets Schwarz. "Did you get Varone's office doctored up okay?" he asked him.

Schwarz stared solemnly back at Bolan. "Sure. That jazzed-up joint was a natural. Never saw such an overdecorated layout. He's rigged good. And I got a twelve-hour recorder with a voice-impulse starter up on the roof of the next building. Bloodbrother was assisting, so he knows where it is. We can slip up there twice a day and change the tapes, and that gives us a twenty-four-hour automatic surveillance on the place."

"Great." Bolan washed down the last of the sandwich with a swallow of coffee. He glanced at his watch. "I'd like to have that first tape before ten this morning. Take Bloodbrother to cover you. Oh, and since Giordano is out of the picture now, maybe you better figure some way to get your gadgets out of his place before someone discovers them. No sense tipping our hand before we just have to."

"I already did that."

Bolan's eyebrows raised.

"These things are too damn hard to come by. I don't leave them laying around in a dead drop."

"My nerves," Andromede said. "I wouldn't have your job between a nympho's tits."

Schwarz smiled. "I enjoy it," he murmured.

Bolan was staring at Fontenelli. "That cop," he mused.

"What cop?" Schwarz asked.

"I was, uh, thinking out loud, I guess," Bolan replied. "Chopper and I had a little encounter with a plainclothes cop out at Tri-Coast tonight."

"Yeah, we heard about it," Andromede said.

"That cop was bad news—plenty bad news, I'm afraid. Did, uh, any of you get a good look at the cops we boxed off the freeway this afternoon?"

The men exchanged glances. None volunteered a reply. "I did," Bolan said, after a moment of silence. "They were right alongside me for a few seconds there, you know. And I had 'em in my rear view for damn near a full minute."

Another short silence followed. Bolan seemed to be lost in thought. Presently, Zitka said, "So?"

"Well, so the cop who was breathing on Chopper and me at Tri-Coast tonight was also in that tail car on the freeway this afternoon."

"What does that prove?" Zitka wanted to know.

"Well now, look—cops are like troops. I mean, a guy in Dog Company is not likely to be found over in a Charlie Company firefight. A cop who's on a routine stakeout over at Giordano's at three in the afternoon isn't likely to be found on a routine investigation out at the edge of Burbank at midnight that same night. They just don't play that way."

"Unless the guy is in some elite squad," Zitka muttered thoughtfully.

"Exactly. And the police response was quick. Damn quick. They were all over that place in no time at all."

"Like they'd been just sitting and waiting for someplace to run to, eh?" Blancanales observed.

Bolan showed him a faint smile. "Yeah. And this cop called me by name."

"Hell, he called *me* Bolan, too," Fontenelli remarked.

"Makes it even a worse case," Bolan replied. "It wasn't a matter of personal recognition. It was a case of expectation. He went there *expecting* to find me."

"Hell, you're a celebrity," Harrington piped up, grinning.

"Goes deeper than that, Guns," Bolan replied. "It looks as though the police have set up some sort of special unit. A unit that is directed squarely against *us*."

"Screw 'em," Fontenelli sneered. "They haven't showed me anything yet."

"We don't get off that easy, Chopper," Bolan said thoughtfully. "It pays to know your opposition. If those people are gearing up to bring us down, then we damn sure have to do some gearing of our own. I don't like it. All of you know what can be accomplished with just a little bit of close-order organization. We've been successful so far because we've been playing it to a cadence count. Now if the cops are playing that same game, then I'd say we'd better come up with a counterpoint."

"The sarge is right," Andromede said. "We need some intelligence. Who's our intelligence officer?" His gaze fell squarely upon Gadgets Schwarz.

Schwarz merely smiled and shrugged his shoulders.

A momentary silence followed; then Loudelk said, "I've tried everything else. I guess I could try infiltrating copsville."

Bolan smiled wanly. "We'd better look at the idea pretty close. Could be a suicide mission."

95

"It'd be just like sending Deadeye to Montgomery," Zitka growled, "to infiltrate the triple K."

Deadeye snickered and rolled his eyes.

"Gadgets and me could figure something," Loudelk insisted stubbornly. His eyes were on Bolan, but he was speaking directly to Schwarz. "If I got you into range, couldn't you come up with something?"

Andromede snapped his fingers and sang a little tune to the words "In the fuzz's hall, we'll give our all, for a bug or two on the men in blue."

"Cut that crap out," Fontenelli growled.

Bolan was returning Loudelk's direct stare. He was thinking about it. "What do you say, Gadgets?" he asked in a barely audible voice.

Schwarz also was thinking about it. "There are several ways to go about it," he replied slowly. "We could monitor their radio frequencies, and that would be the safest and the easiest, but . . ."

"But?" Bolan prompted.

"Well we really do need to have a monitor on their radio nets, but it will take some inside work to just find out what those frequencies are."

"All right, consider that as an objective," Bolan agreed. "We want their radio frequencies. That should be an easy mark. Any radio amateur could probably give us that. But they probably have some special radio net for their elite unit. We'll need that, above all. Go on, Gadgets."

Okay, that would be in the nature of just routine intelligence. These people don't tell their secrets over the radio, though, bet on that. So we need some way to monitor their telephone conversations, their official discussions, and their bull sessions. That means we have to get inside or . . ."

"Or what?"

"If this elite squad has a . . . well, they have to have, don't they? A honcho, a guy in charge. We

96

need to know who he is and where his headquarters are located."

"The L.A. cops operate out of the Hall of Justice, don't they?" Harrington put in.

"I don't mean just the damn building," Schwarz said. "I mean a particular room or office."

"You're really serious?" Fontenelli asked. "You'd try to get in there and plant bugs, right in the damn police station?"

"That may not be necessary," Schwarz replied. "I might be able to use a directional mike."

Bolan and Zitka exchanged thoughtful glances.

"I made a pickup once from a quarter mile," Schwarz told them. "Of course, it was in quiet countryside. Noise level is much higher in a city like L.A., with a lot of diffusion of sound waves. Generally, without too much diffusion, you can trap a sound from anything you can see."

Bolan sighed. "Give it a try, Gadgets. You and Brother get down there as soon as you feel ready and scout the layout. See what you can figure out, but don't make any actual move until I've reviewed your plan. We'll give this a top priority, and we make no further hits until our intelligence apparatus is functioning. While you're out, pick up that tape from the Varone drop. I'll want to know his reactions to tonight's hit." He showed Loudelk a grim smile. "I'm depending on your instincts, Brother, to keep this play safe. If it can't be done without undue risk, we'll just get along without it. Okay?"

Loudelk smiled. "Okay."

"I'll have to build a mike," Schwarz added.

"You have all the stuff you need?"

"I think so. If not, I can pick up what I need in any electronics shop."

Bolan shifted his gaze to Blancanales. "We've used the vehicles long enough, Politician," he said crisply. "Better drop them and get some more. Be very discreet. Include my 'Vette—get me something else. Anything that's got some fire. Maybe a Porsche, eh?"

"You don't mean the horse, too?" Blancanales asked, frowning.

"No, but see what you can do about some new paint and decals. What about license tags?"

"No problem there." They're scared to death you were going to make me rig up a new horse."

Bolan chuckled. "We might have to drop the horse idea entirely after another strike or two. They're bound to tumble to it sooner or later, and then that big mother becomes a dead liability. Be thinking about a new gimmick."

Blancanales' frown deepened. "My nightmares are gettin' worse all the time," he groused.

The remark produced laughter from around the room. Andromede leaned over to place a hand on the Politician's shoulder and loudly announced, "My nerves, man, I wouldn't have your job—"

"Yeah I know," Blancanales sourly interrupted, "Between a nympho's tits."

"No, I was going to say, in a confession booth in a cathouse."

When the good-humored eruption had quieted, Andromede added, "And I'm ready for some R and R."

Bolan was studying his watch. "Well, it's getting on to four o'clock," he said. "I can't offer you much in the way of recreation, but it is time for a bit of rest. Let's all turn in. Eight o'clock reveille."

"Four *hours!*—I'm losin' my *powers!*" Andromede groaned.

"I'm gonna shove that poetry right up your ass one o' these days," Fontenelli growled good-naturedly.

"Only with your nose, bro," Andromede replied.

98

He tossed a playful punch that missed Fontenelli by a foot, then danced lightly away, shadow boxing across the room and into the hallway.

Bolan sighed and got to his feet. He was having second thoughts about this death squad bit. The responsibility for these men's lives and fortunes was beginning to weigh heavily upon him. He was using them, and he knew it, and the knowledge bothered him. Bolan had a consecrated interest in this war upon the Mafia. These men did not. What right had he to involve them in this life-and-death business?

Deadeye Washington had also risen to his feet and was now walking beside Bolan toward the hall to the bedrooms. He seemed to sense Bolan's feelings. "These guys are here 'cause there's really noplace else they'd rather be," he told Bolan in a soft drawl.

"Maybe you're right," Bolan murmured.

"Sure I'm right. Some men just live to die, 'cause they're already dead."

"Are you already dead, Deadeye?" Bolan asked, looking at the big Negro with some surprise.

"This black man? Sure, man. I was born dead. And I'm still borning."

It was not a particularly comforting idea for Bolan to take into his dreams.

Chapter Nine

ONE LITTLE INDIAN

"Okay, so Bolan turned up a new gangland front for us," Captain Braddock said wearily. His manner was clearly one of irritation as he glared at his young detail leader, Sergeant Carl Lyons. "So what do we do—hang a Legion of Merit around his neck?"

Lyons responded with an embarrassed smile. "I merely pointed out that his presence here isn't entirely negative," the sergeant replied. His gaze wavered, broke, and shifted to Lieutenant Rickert. He found little comfort there.

"Looks like Bolan's found a convert," the lieutenant sneered. "Listen, kid, don't get your wires crossed. This guy and his drill team are the most vicious threat to hit this city in my memory. Don't go getting any romantic ideas."

"Who is he a threat to?" Lyons replied stubbornly. "The only people I've seen hurting so far are those who should be hurting. Hell, I—"

"That's enough of that!" Braddock snapped. "I don't want any intellectual discussions around here about the debits and credits of Mack Bolan. It's nonsense, utter damn nonsense, and I'll release you, Sergeant, from Hardcase duty, effective immediately, if that is your wish."

"That is not my wish." Lyons clipped back. "My wish is to see Mack Bolan behind bars." His anger seemed to evaporate in a flash. He raised a smile to the captain and added, "I'll bet you an evening on the Strip that I'm the man who brings him in."

Braddock's face brightened. "You're on. You want a piece of this action, Charlie?"

Rickert smiled and shook his head. "I'm just a cop, doing a cop's job," he said. "I don't make book on anything that might happen. But you're going to win that bet, Tim. Wet-behind-the-ears, here, won't get within hailing distance of Bolan. The word is out, all over town. My informants tell me that Mack Bolan is as good as dead."

"What do you mean, Charlie?" Braddock was wearing a troubled frown.

Rickert spread his hands in a delicate gesture. "Only that the Mafia generals are taking over the action, that's all."

"I'm still not sure I understand what you're saying."

"According to the words I'm getting, the family has not been overly worried about Bolan. They put out a hundred-thou open contract and forgot about him. You know what an open contract means. Anybody can collect—anybody who can bring in Bolan's scalp. Well . . . now the family is getting worried. The bounty hunters have been striking out. They can't even get a finger on the guy, and meantime he's chopping hell out of the local nephews. So they're taking over the action. It probably means a hot war."

"So why the roundabout way of letting me in on it?" Braddock snapped. "Hell, Rickert, do you know what you're saying? Gang war, that's what! Where did you get this information?"

Rickert was smiling, unruffled by the hostility of Braddock's tone. "It's all in my report, Tim. It's lying right there on your desk."

The captain's harsh glare snapped down to the desk. "Okay, so I'm behind in my reading," he growled.

"Figured you were," Rickert observed. He was smiling. "Tell you what. I'll break a long time M.O. I'll make some book on this case. If Mack Bolan is not lying in a drawer of the morgue within seventy-two hours, I'll give you both an evening on the Strip."

"I, uh, don't like to bet on life and death," Braddock replied quietly.

Lyons scraped to his feet. "Me either. Well, it's past noon and all's quiet. I'm due back on the streets at six. I'm going home and get some rest, if that's okay."

Braddock gave Lyons an absent-minded nod. Obviously his mind was occupied with the information Rickert had just dropped. The sergeant's departure was hardly noticed. Rickert was toying with a paperweight. "That kid will make a pretty good cop if he ever grows up," he said.

Braddock ignored the comment. "We're in trouble, Charlie," he declared.

"I know it."

"We are not one inch closer to Bolan than we were this time yesterday."

"I know that, too."

Braddock scratched his forehead and rocked back in his chair. "Gang war, eh?"

"Worse than that. Little Vietnam."

"We've got to stop it. Before it gets started. Today. Now."

Rickert smiled genially. "Sure, but how?"

"Let's go talk to the chief."

"What about?"

Braddock's breath whooshed out in a heavy sigh. "If we can't reach Bolan, we'll just have to reason with the other side. It's roundup time, Charlie."

"Aw hell, Tim." Rickert's geniality had taken a rapid departure. "You're not talking about a *Mafia* roundup."

"Sure I am." Braddock rocked forward in the chair and depressed a button on the intercom. "See if the chief's in," he said tiredly into the interoffice

102

communicator. "If he is, get me an open door. I have to discuss an urgent development in Hardcase, soonest possible."

A male voice acknowledged the instructions. Rickert was lighting a cigarette. "It's a useless exercise, Tim," he said heavily. "We don't have a damned thing to even book them on, and you know it. Their lawyers will be down here with writs before we can get the doors closed."

"So we'll bust them again an hour later, and we'll keep on busting them every hour on the hour until we can get Bolan on ice. At least it'll keep them off-balance and prevent them from launching any sort of armed offensive."

"But we'll be playing right into Bolan's hands," Rickert said nervously. "We don't have a line on every nephew in this town. The ones we don't get will be ripe meat for Bolan's butchers."

"Well, goddammit, I've got no great bleeding heart for Bolan, Charlie—but I sure as hell don't fancy myself as the Mafia's father protector, either, for God's sake. Bolan will get to a few of them. He's doing it anyway. So that's a hell of a sight better than having our streets running blood. Hell."

"I think it would be a mistake," Rickert persisted bitterly. "First thing you know, we *will* be hanging a Legion of Merit around Bolan's neck."

"One thing you have to learn, Charlie," Braddock snapped. "That's when to turn off the just-plain-cop and turn on the twentieth century." His gaze flicked past Rickert, to take in the lean figure of a man who had just stepped into his doorway. The man was deeply tanned, had very prominent cheekbones, and was neatly dressed in an opened-neck white shirt and slacks. "Yes?" Braddock asked, acknowledging the visitor's presence.

"Are you Captain Braddock?" the man asked.

Braddock nodded. "Yes, I am."

"They sent me up here. I was in Hollywood last night, and saw these men running out of this building, see. I saw in the papers this morning—"

"Right down the hall, please. First door on the left."

"Sir?"

"You want to make eyewitness report on the robbery at the Tri-Coast Studios, don't you?"

"Yes sir. They sent me up here."

"Please go into the large room just down the hall, first door on your left. They'll take your statement there. And thank you for coming in."

"Are you sure?" The man was peering uncertainly along the corridor, standing half-in and half-out of Braddock's doorway.

"What?" Braddock was becoming impatient.

"Well, I passed that room. There's radios and stuff in there. I just want to report—"

"That's the proper place to give your statement, sir. Just walk right in and tell the man at the desk why you're here."

The man smiled. "Well . . . okay."

"Thank you, sir," the captain said, forcing a smile.

The man moved uncertainly down the hall. Rickert was wearing a strained smile. "That's twentieth century, eh? Saying 'sir' to a wetback?"

"That's right," Braddock replied through tight lips. "A citizen is a citizen, and every one of them rates a 'sir' in this building—until they're booked, anyway. And he wasn't a wetback. I'd say Cherokee or Navajo. That's about as *citizen* as you can get."

"An *Indian*?" Rickert asked, slowly stiffening upright in his chair.

The two men locked eyes for a tense instant. Braddock half-rose from his seat, then settled back with an embarrassed grin. "Hell, Charlie, you made my blood run cold for a second there," he said.

Rickert chuckled. "Goes to show how subjective you can get on these twenty-four-hour cases," he replied. He leaned forward to crush out his cigarette. "What the hell would Bolan's Indian be doing up here at Hardcase Central?"

"Go ask him," Braddock suggested, grinning.

"Ask him yourself, you're the coordinator," Rickert replied, entirely satisfied with the change of atmosphere in the captain's office. He had over reacted to Braddock's decision for a Mafia drag, he realized, and he had needed that little diversion. Thank God for stumbling, wide-eyed, dumb-ass "citizens" who, lost or not, were determined to do their civic duty. Bolan's (ha-ha) Indian had pulled the twenty-four-hour cop's fat out of the fire. For the moment, at any rate.

Down the hall, a bronzed man with prominent cheekbones was performing a citizen's duty, filing a written eyewitness report of a crime—and mentally filing an unwritten eyewitness report on the plan and layout of Captain Braddock's control room. Bolan's Indian had plenty to do at Hardcase Central.

Chapter Ten

THE SOFT SELL

"A directional mike is out of the question," Schwarz reported glumly. "It's a hard building, any way you look at it."

"Internal security is a loose goose, though," Loudelk told Bolan. He tossed a small notebook onto Bolan's lap. "They call the operation *Hardcase*. The names of the detail leaders and their areas are in the notes there. Got that from a duty roster pinned to a bulletin board in their control room." He withdrew a three-by-five card from his hip pocket and waved it gently in front of Bolan's eyes. "And guess what this is. Phone numbers and radio frequencies on the front, code words on the back." He produced a folded paper from his shirt pocket and added it to the loot on Bolan's lap. "And this is an area map, showing zones of responsibility for the various details."

Bolan was wearing a broad grin. "Bloodbrother, you're a master craftsman," he said.

"Place was wide open. I just walked in and picked it up. This Braddock, the cop in charge, looks more like a judge than a cop. He's hard, though, and the other cops respect him. They call him Big Tim. Behind his back, anyway. His office adjoins their control room. Floor plan's in the notebook. They're running a military operation there, Sarge. I'd say they want us real bad."

Bolan nodded, the grin still in place. His eyes were traveling down the list of radio frequencies printed on the card. "Can you cover these frequencies, Gadgets?" he asked.

"Yeah, but I'll have to get some more gear. I'll

need some cash. I'd say . . . oh, about at least two thousand. If you want to cover all those at the same time."

"Money is no object," Bolan replied. "What better use for Mafia green, eh? Draw what you need from Politician. Need any help?"

Schwarz shook his head in a decided negative. "I shop better by m'self," he said.

"Okay, but play it cautious. Don't excite anyone's curiosity. Brother, you cover him, separate vehicles, SOP. From this moment forward, no one leaves base camp without a cover man."

"Let's chow up first," Loudelk suggested, his eyes on Schwarz. The electronics man nodded, and they went off together toward the kitchen.

Schwarz halted in the doorway and turned back to Bolan. "You get anything worthwhile from that tape I sent back?"

"Plenty," Bolan assured him. "Chopper and Gunsmoke are out reconning a couple of leads right now." He got to his feet and strolled over to join Schwarz in the doorway. "And a special little chunk of dynamite I saved for myself. I didn't know quite how to use it, but now . . . well, I believe Loudelk's intelligence has shown me the way. Listen, Gadgets, get those radio monitors set up just as soon as possible. They're going to be a hell of a weapon for us." He started to walk away, then whirled back and added, "And listen—I don't care how much it costs—set up a mobile capability. Maybe we can use the horse as a rolling command post. You know what I'm thinking of?"

Schwarz was smiling with bright enthusiasm. "I know exactly what you're thinking of. I dunno if I can do it in one day, though."

Bolan slapped him on the rear and said, "Sure you can. A genius can do anything."

Schwarz grinned and went on into the kitchen.

Bolan walked back across the big room and onto the patio. Deadeye Washington was out there, working over his sniper piece with a cleaning cloth. "You ate yet?" Bolan asked him.

Washington nodded solemnly. "If you can call a TV Dinner eating," he replied. "When we gonna get a cook around here?"

Bolan ignored the question. "We have work. You're on me. Side-arm only, street clothes. Meet me out front in ten minutes."

Washington sighed and grunted up out of the chair. "Good thing," he said, chuckling. "Gettin' lazy. Been about twelve hours since I sweated bird turds."

Carl Lyons pulled his car into the driveway of the modest tract home, thoughtfully eyed the sack of groceries on the seat beside him, and mentally ran over the list of items Janie had asked him to buy. He had detoured via the barber shop for a quick trim, where he had further dwadled over some television replays of the latest Rams games, and unavoidably the shopping list had become somewhat blurred in his memory. He poked absently into the sack, hoping he hadn't forgotten anything. He needed to lie down for at least an hour before dinner and then return to duty. He certainly had no desire to spend the balance of his free time running back and forth to the supermarket.

The young policeman stepped out of the car, dragging the sack with him and then swinging it under one arm. He kicked the door shut and headed up the walk to the kitchen door, pausing momentarily to reposition a child's tricycle that was blocking the way.

His wife was standing at the open door of the refrigerator, peering into its depths with a perplexed frown. This was the way Lyons appreciated Janie best—candid, off-guard, unaware of her husband's observation. Not that she exhibited an affected manner in his presence; it was just that she had a special quality that shone more brightly in personal solitude. She looked up and caught him gazing at her with a special quality of his own. The luminous eyes flashed in a startled smile, and she said, "Thought you were either lost or arrested. You've been gone for an hour and a half."

"Haircut," he explained, fanning the back of his head with an open palm. He placed the sack on the drainboard. "I probably forgot something."

Janie was still standing at the open refrigerator. "I could have sworn we had a bottle of Seven-Up," she said.

"Now that wasn't on the list, Janie," Lyons declared defensively.

She smiled. "Go tell it to your friend in there. How am I going to mix him a drink if we have no mix? Huh, Mr. Detective?"

"What friend?" Lyons asked, frowning.

"Mr. Mac-something-or-other. He said you were expecting him. Aren't you expecting him?" She slammed the refrigerator door, reading the expression on her husband's face. "These salesmen!" she exclaimed in controlled fury. "They'll try *any-thing* to get in the door. Go in there and tell him we don't want a thing, not a thing, unless he has an instant money tree for nothing down and nothing a week. *You* tell him. *I* have to get supper."

Lyons was already moving through the swinging door and along the short hallway. He hesitated at the archway into the living room. A tall man in a conservatively tailored suit stood at the window, his back to Lyons. Neatly trimmed blond hair shimmered in the sunlight filtering through the window. Lyons's four-year-old son, Tommy, was

109

holding the man's hand and pointing to something in the yard.

The man turned slowly to acknowledge Lyon's entrance, a faint smile twisting at his lips. "We meet again," he said softly. "Fine boy you have here." He ruffled Tommy's hair with a gentle hand. "He was just telling me about your mole problem. You'd think, in this atomic age, someone would have come up with a sure cure for lawn pests."

Lyons's heart was thundering in his ears. He glanced at his son, who was tugging trustingly at the man's fingers, and his mouth went dry. "Mama needs you in the kitchen, Tommy," he croaked.

The boy stared at his father for a rebellious moment, then scowled unhappily and marched obediently out of the room. The tall man spread his hands in front of him, palms down, as if to show that they were empty and unthreatening.

"What the hell are you doing here, Bolan?" Lyons snarled in a tightly controlled voice.

"A brief truce, like last night. In the interests of justice."

"Last night was a fluke! You'll never walk away from me again, Bolan."

"Don't go off half-cocked," Bolan warned softly. "I have no wish to bring warfare into your home." His eyes flicked toward the kitchen door. "Those are nice people in there. Let's keep it peaceful."

Lyons was angry enough to spit brimstone. "You've got a goddamned nerve, coming into *my* house. All right, Bolan. Let's hear what's on your mind?"

Bolan's eyes swept to a small plastic case resting on a table near the window. "I brought along a tape player. I want you to listen to a recording we made from a drop in Varone's Hollywood apartment."

110

"Why?" Lyons was developing interest despite himself.

"I want to see if you can identify a cop, from his first name and his voice."

"Again, why?"

"Because *this* cop is on the Mafia payroll."

A brief silence ensued; then: "But why do you bring it to me? Just because I froze once doesn't mean I've become your bosom buddy. Why me?"

"Because I figure any good cop will want to uncover a bad one. And I can't very well walk into the Hall of Justice with it, can I?" Bolan's eyes flicked once again to the kitchen door. "You *are* a good cop, aren't you, Lyons?"

The detective's lips twitched under a strongly guarded emotion. "All right. Play your tape. You want to sit down?"

"Thanks, I'll stand." Bolan twisted to one side to rest his hands on the tape player. "It's best that I stay right here in the window. My outside man would get nervous if I moved out of his sight."

"You think of it all, don't you?"

A faint smile played on Bolan's face. "Have to," he replied. "It's the only way I stay alive. You should try playing fox over the hill someday, with yourself as the fox."

"Don't cry on *my* shoulder, Bolan. You're the guy who blew the whistle that started the game."

"See any tears?" Bolan asked pleasantly. "I was just apologizing for busting into your home this way."

"I believe you *are* apologizing," Lyons admitted grudgingly.

Bolan loked surprised. "I am." He pushed a control at the front of the player. "I made a copy of the pertinent part of our tape and put it in a cartridge for you." He adjusted the volume control.

"You'll have to listen closely. There's a bit of background noise here and there."

The little tape player had surprisingly good tonal quality. A thick voice swelled up from the tiny speaker, saying, "How the *hell* did they get onto me? How did they know? You find out! You hear me? That's what you're getting paid for!"

A reedy, sneering voice came in, following a short pause. "Don't remind me of my sins, Varone. Don't get too shook up, either. We'll have this guy on ice soon enough."

Lyons's eyes flared wide, then narrowed speculatively. He moved closer to the tape player, hardly breathing, listening intently to the damning conversation. His eyes swiveled to Bolan moments later, his lips twisting with disgust as the thick voice whined, "We ain't been giving you two grand a month to just—"

It was a short recording. When it was finished, Lyons turned the machine off, dropped into a chair facing Bolan, and said, "That put a ball of mush right in the pit of my guts."

"You know the guy?"

Lyons was staring levelly at Bolan's belt buckle. He nodded his head in silent affirmation.

Bolan slowly brought out a package of cigarettes, lit one, and offered the pack to Lyons. The policeman ignored the offer. Bolan returned the pack to his pocket, slowly exhaled, and said, "It's Lieutenant Charlie Rickert, isn't it?"

"Where are you getting these names?" Lyons snapped. "Where'd you get *mine*? How did you—?" He smiled suddenly, with the lips only, and clamped his mouth shut. "I'm not running a private agency here, Bolan," he continued in a more pleasant tone. "Don't you ever come here again. The next time I see you, I'll do all my talking with my gun. Now get out of here."

"Don't take it all out on me," Bolan replied mildly. "I just made the recording. I didn't say the words." He was moving toward the door. "I'll leave the player with you. Give my regards to your lovely wife."

"Leave my wife—"

"Okay, okay. You really better do something about those moles, though. They're playing hell with your lawn." He smiled, stepped through the door, and closed it lightly behind him.

Lyons stepped quickly to the window. Already the bold bastard was moving past the corner of the hedges and out of sight. Lyons sighed, a grim smile playing at his lips.

Janie came through the swinging door at that instant and cautiously poked her head around the corner. "I see you got rid of him," she said.

"Yeah, but I have a feeling it's not for long," he replied. He raised a hand to the back of his neck and squeezed down strongly on the bunched muscles.

"You didn't *buy* anything from him, I hope," his wife wailed.

"Yeah," he said softly. "Yeah, I'm afraid I bought quite a bit."

Chapter Eleven

SNEAK PREVIEW

The horse was behind the camouflage netting when Bolan and Washington returned to the base camp, and the big vehicle was the object of multiple attentions. Hoffower and Loudelk were spraying the van with a fast-drying paint. Fontenelli was crawling about on the roof with an electric drill. Blancanales and Zitka were struggling with a large framework of wood shelving, being arm waved through the huge doors by Schwarz.

Schwarz spotted Bolan's approach. He stepped through the shelf framing and swung down off the tailgate, grinning at Bolan in quiet exuberance. "We're almost set," he announced. "I got all solid-state, self-contained gear. All we have to do now is get it set in the racks, install the antenna mast, run a few connections—and we're in business."

"The antenna problem is my biggest worry," Bolan told him, critically eyeing the big rig. "With all those things sticking up out of there, it's going to look suspect as hell."

"I already thought of that," Schwarz assured him. "No sweat. I'm running just one whip, horizontal along the roof, with couplings per set. That will be the only thing showing, and it'll be hardly noticeable. Chopper is punching me some holes, and I'm running the antenna leads along the inside to each coupling."

"I'm not sure I understand that." Bolan grinned. "But I'll take your word for it. Good show, Gadgets. How much longer before you're finished?"

"Couple hours, at the most. It'll work, Sarge."

Bolan slapped him on the shoulder and went on

to the house. He found Harrington and Washington conversing in low tones on the patio. Harrington raised his voice, lifting it toward Bolan, and announced, "Yeah, man, we had a swingin' afternoon. That Varone cat has his fingers in just about everything."

Bolan pulled a chair away from the patio table, turned it around, and settled onto it in a straddling movement, his arms draped across the backrest. "Tell me about it," he said, alertly interested.

Harrington did likewise, bouncing his chair about to directly face Bolan. "First off," he said intently, "I get the idea that even his recording outfit is slightly off-color. You know what a 'cover' is, in record talk?"

Bolan shook his head in a negative response.

"Well, some outfit comes out with a pretty good record, see, and they plug hell out of it—promotion, you know, a bit of oil to the deejays here and there—you know the routine. The thing starts climbing in the sales charts, hits the top forty, and it looks like it's going all the way. A hit, see? So I guess it's a pretty much accepted practice for other companies to bring out a record just like it—same song, see. This is called covering. You could think of it as legitimate competition—except that the outfit that brought the thing out in the first place has took all the risks and spent all this money in plugging and promoting."

"I'm following," Bolan assured him.

"Well—Tri-Coast never puts out anything *but* covers. They call it covering, I call it stealing. They use the exact same arrangements, never change a damn note. And here's the worse part—they pick up these starvin' kids who are trying to make it big out here in Hollywood, see, pay 'em a damn thin fee for cutting the record, and that's it. The artists never make another penny off that

115

record, no matter how many it sells, and Varone is rolling in profit. He's the worse kind of rat, Mack—he's exploiting kids, the rock groups and folk singers who are just dying for that big chance. He's giving them crumbs and making a killing for himself."

"But nothing illegal," Bolan observed quietly.

"Not that anyone could say for certain. There's talk that his distributor leans pretty hard on deejays and the small record shops. Payola for the deejays and kickbacks to the record shops if they sell a certain quota. I don't know if there's a law against that or not."

"Okay, how about the other activities?"

Harrington put on a grim smile. "*Now* we're getting to the nitty-gritty. He's pushing everything, from girls to acid. I get the idea he's a silent honcho in a big modeling agency out on Wilshire. He's also collecting money from a guy who has an office up on the Strip, calls himself a theatrical agent. The only flesh he peddles, though, is girl flesh. Showgirls, mostly, strippers and that type. And I smell a call-girl operation, loud and clear."

Bolan nodded his head. "You said something about acid."

"Yeah, hell, the whole bit. Grass, speed, acid, goofballs, the big H—everything that kicks or purrs."

"How do you know?"

Harrington grinned. "I found someone who shared his bed and board for a while."

Bolan's eyebrows rose. "A girl?"

"Yeah. And *what* a girl. All boobs and butt, beautiful as a rose and just about as brainless."

"She knows quite a bit about Varone's operations?"

Harrington shrugged. "In a general sort of way. You can never tell about these dumb ones. How

116

much detail they know, I mean. She came in to record a cover for Varone 'bout three months ago, then stayed on to keep his bed warm for a few weeks. Lived right there in his apartment above the recording studios. Then he got tired of her and showed her the way out." A faint smile briefly lighted Harrington's face. "She's like a damn recorder herself, Mack. Push one button and she records. Push another and she plays back. I can't figure a guy like Varone letting her learn that much, then turning her loose on the world. Unless he just figured she was too damn dumb to have learned anything about him. She *is* dumb, Mack. But all her mental energies seem to work through her memory cells. No kidding, she's like a damn tape recorder."

"Could you find her again?"

"Sure," Harrington said, smiling. "You want to talk to her?"

"Maybe." Bolan was staring fixedly at his fingertips. "What was Varone doing today?"

"Busy-busy," Harrington replied. "Chopper has the log. We split off at two o'clock. He stayed on Varone while I checked out the other stuff."

Bolan nodded, his face devoid of expression. "I'll get with Chopper for the details. What impression did you get, Guns—from what Chopper told you, I mean?"

"About Varone? I'd say he's running scared. He made about six stops, one of 'em at a big joint up in Beverly Hills. Stayed in there about twenty minutes. And then he drove all the way down to San Pedro."

"Who'd he see there?"

Harrington shrugged. "Chopper said he went into this warehouse on the waterfront. Stayed about five minutes, then bugged straight home."

Bolan got to his feet. "I'd better talk to Chopper. Sounds like things are shaping up. Deadeye?"

"Yeah?" Washington had been listening attentively to the conversation. He was now grinning broadly at Bolan, leaning forward to intercept his words.

"Get ready for a fire mission. You and me. Take my big sniper down to the range and sight it in up to 300 yards. Give me 'scope calibrations for every hundred feet. Better do the same for yours if you haven't already."

Washington was all smiles. "Hot damn," he said.

"Will I be in this one?" Harrington asked.

"You bet you will. You and Chopper will flank us."

"Where's the hit?"

"I'll have to talk to Chopper before I'm sure. But from what you've told me, along with what I got from Gadget's tape, it looks like Beverly Hills."

"The big joint?"

Bolan nodded. "The big joint. Varone's been trying to set up a family council. Beverly Hills sounds like the place. I'll take Zitter and Bloodbrother out there for a recon while we still have some daylight."

Bolan left them and headed for the horse to speak with Chopper. Harrington looked at Washington and said, "He doesn't believe in sitting around, does he?"

"I was tellin' you what that soul did this afternoon," Washington said, lowering his voice conspiratorially. "So, see—he just walked up to that policeman's house and rung the doorbell. I see him in there talking to the little boy. Then the cop gets there, and Mack is standin' there in the window, talkin' to him like a soul brother—cool, see, like egg custard on a summer day, and then he . . ."

118

Deadeye Washington had found something to believe in. He believed in Mack Bolan's guts.

Sergeant Carl Lyons picked up his detail assignment at the operations center, then stepped hesitantly into Captain Braddock's office. The captain was having a desk-top dinner of coffee and sandwiches. He looked up with a scowl. "Something on your mind, Carl?" he asked.

Lyons stood just inside the doorway. "I didn't see Rickert's name on the board," he replied. "Wondering if he's on tonight."

"He's on a special," Braddock growled. He distastefully eyed a sandwich, lifting a coffee cup to his lips instead.

A surge of emotion had briefly illuminated Lyons's face. "Undercover?" he asked tautly.

Braddock's eyes smiled across the rim of the cup, as though he were visualizing the unlikely suggestion. "Rickert's a bit old for intrigue," he replied. "What is it, Carl?"

"Oh, it's a . . . personal matter. What's coming off, Captain? The assignments are all shuffled."

Braddock stared at his young sergeant for a moment; then he smiled and said, "Close the door and come on in, Carl. You have a moment, don't you?"

Lyons nodded and advanced into the office, taking a chair at the front of the desk.

"Don't even mention this to the men of your detail," Braddock told him. "We are setting the wheels in motion for a Mafia dragnet, scheduled for first thing tomorrow. It's a harassment move, pure and simple, and the only object is to prevent the buildup of a Mafia army in response to the Bolan threat. We will be altering the Hardcase strategy also, and you'll be kept abreast of developments in that area. Is Bolan getting to you, Carl?"

119

Lyons was thrown temporarily off-guard by the sudden question. "I don't . . . how do you mean?"

"What did you want to see Rickert about?"

"Is he working the details of the dragnet?"

"How come you answer every one of my questions with one of your own?"

Lyons colored and cleared his throat. "That son of a bitch was at my house today."

"What son of a bitch?"

"Bolan."

A heavy silence descended. Presently, Braddock said, "It took you long enough to tell me about it."

"I wanted to see Rickert first."

"Why?"

"Look, Captain, he just walked right into my house. My son entertained him in the living room while Janie was trying to rustle him up something to drink!"

"No, dammit—Bolan!"

Another silence; then: "I can understand how you feel, Carl. Look, we'll put a man on your house. Next time he—"

"He won't be back. He sat there and waited for me. I talked to him. He did what he came to do, and he left."

"I see. No—I don't see. Just like that? He left?"

Lyons curtly nodded his head. "Damn right. I wasn't about to risk a gunfight. Not with Janie and Tommy fifteen feet away."

"All right. There are various questions that immediately come to my mind, but for openers, what did he come to do?"

Lyons glared steadily into his superior's eyes for a tense moment; then he wordlessly got to his feet, walked out of the office, and returned an instant later carrying a small plastic case. "Something here I want you to listen to," he announced in a choked voice. "Make your own conclusions. I've already made mine."

Zeno Varone's voice rasped through the telephone line in a threatening snarl. "Well by God, Charlie, you just better put a spike in it, that's all I can say. Just what the hell you think your job *is*, anyway?"

"Don't talk like a total ass," Rickert came back in an angry near whisper. "This isn't anything I can control. It's value enough that I'm even able to tip you to it."

"We won't stand still for no rousting, Charlie."

"And just what in hell do you think you can do about it?" responded the lieutenant's infuriated whisper.

"I'll tell you what we can do about it! We'll slap 'em with so many false-arrest suits, they'll—"

"Then you'll have to do your slapping from a cell! I'm telling you, they are beginning the roundup at eight tomorrow morning. Now you take it from there!" An abrupt click and a hum announced the disconnection.

Varone shouted into the hum, "You're not too goddamn important to get your name on a contract, Rickert! Rickert? If you hung up on me you sonnabitch, I swear, I'll . . ." A short pause, then: "The sonnabitch hung up on me."

Bolan smiled at Loudelk and turned off the recorder. "Glad we stopped by to pick this up," he said. "Stop at the next phone. I want to make a call."

Loudelk nodded and angled into the outside lane of traffic. At the next intersection, he swung into a service station and halted the car alongside a telephone booth.

Bolan dropped his dime through the slot and

dialed the number of the police switchboard. "It's urgent that I speak with Lieutenant Charlie Rickert," he told the switchboard operator.

"Just a moment, please."

"He's on the Tim Braddock detail, Hardcase."

The word seemed to be a magic key. "Oh, yes, just a . . . ringing."

Bolan thanked the operator, smiling grimly at Loudelk through the glass of the booth. A deep male voice answered the first ring. "Hardcase."

"Urgent for Charlie Rickert," Bolan responded. "He said I should call him here."

"Just a sec. He's on special. I'll get that number."

"Thanks." Bolan winked at Loudelk.

The voice returned to the line almost immediately. "Hang on, I'm going to flash the operator."

"Okay."

The operator responded on the third click. "Transfer this call to thirty-seven-eleven," the officer instructed.

Bolan again waited while the new connection was being made. A female voice answered. "Urgent for Charlie Rickert," Bolan said.

"Just a moment, please."

Bolan hummed a tune under his breath. "Who is calling please?" the woman asked a moment later.

"It's a hardcase," Bolan said.

"Rickert here," announced a surly voice, after another brief wait.

"Rickert, this is Mack Bolan."

"Yeah, well this is Little Annie Fannie. I don't have time for—"

"Shut up and listen to me. This is Bolan. I'm hitting your buddies tonight."

A short silence later, Rickert said, "On the level? This is really who you say?"

"I don't have time for games either, Rickert."

"Okay. So now just tell me when and where

you're hitting so we can be sure to stay out of your way. What is this? What do you want?"

"I just want to play a tape for you, Rickert. It will be delivered to Braddock first thing in the morning, but I thought I'd give you a sneak performance. You listening?"

"I'm listening."

Bolan touched the rewind button on the recorder, then punched the playback control and snuggled the telephone mouthpiece against the recorder's speaker. He let it run for about thirty seconds, grinning at Loudelk all the while, then stopped the recorder and returned the telephone instrument to his ear. "How'd you like the sneak preview?" he asked in a cold voice. "Pretty sneaky, eh?"

The telephone line was silent. Bolan jiggled the hook, and the switchboard operator came on. "Your party disconnected, sir," she announced. "Do you want me to ring back?"

"No, that's okay," Bolan said, grinning into the mouthpiece. "I guess it's a permanent disconnect. Thank you, operator."

He left the booth and returned to the car. "How'd he take it?" Loudelk asked, smiling.

"He took it hard," Bolan replied. "And . . . I think he took it on the lam."

Chapter Twelve

THE SQUEEZE

"All right, here's the situation," Bolan told the assembled Death Squad. "The pressure is building, strong and fast. The local Maffianos are in a state of general alarm. They're using the pattern I've been expecting them to all along, closing ranks and making preparations to crush us the next time we show ourselves. It's Vanh Duc all over again, but with a troubling difference. That difference has been created by the police interest in this operation. The pressure is on the cops, too, and they're trying their best to lower the boom on us. So we have to worry about two fronts. There's also another item that's liable to throw us a curve. The cops are worried about the Mafia buildup. They view this whole thing as a sort of gang war that could spill out onto their streets at any moment. So they've added a bit of spice to the pot. They've decided to begin a harassment campaign that will keep the Mafia off-balance and unable to wage warfare. Okay—so the word has been leaked to the Mafia. They know that the cops are going to begin rounding them up first thing tomorrow."

"What effect will this have on our plans?" Zitka asked.

"I don't know for sure," Bolan replied, frowning. "I do know, though, that our success depends on getting our job done at the quickest possible pace and getting the hell out of this area. L.A. has about the toughest police department in the nation, and when these guys gear up for you, you can bet that your days are numbered. Two immediate effects, or possiblities, that I can see. Either we'll get knocked off our pace as a result of the police interference or else the Mafia will go into hiding or take a trip or something until the heat's off. Either move will defeat us, or at least defeat our objectives."

"We can lay low, too, can't we?" Andromede said.

"Not around here," Bolan quickly replied. "We can't afford to give the L.A. cops that kind of time-factor to work with. Like I said, these guys know their business. Given enough time, they'll find us and they'll nail us. I had allowed five days for this L.A. operation, and that's all. We've already used two."

"What are you getting at, Mack?" Zitka asked worriedly.

"Well . . ." Bolan scratched his forehead. "Tonight might be our last chance for a grand slammer. I'd say twenty-four hours at the very most. There's too much working against us now."

"You're saying it's a full-dress Vanh Duc tonight, then?"

Bolan soberly nodded his head. "Either that or a full abort."

"Whatta you mean, a full abort?" Fontenelli growled.

Bolan's eyes fell on Blancanales. "What's the take so far, Politician?"

Blancanales coughed, smiled, and said, "In round figures, the grand total is $147,000."

"Okay," Bolan said. "That isn't nearly enough to make all of you independently wealthy, but it's a better stake than you had forty-eight hours ago. If you decide to dissolve the operation here and now, I'll throw the kitty into the split."

"What're you talking about, dissolve the operation?" Andromede said quietly. "Who wants to dissolve the operation?"

125

"It might be best," Blancanales observed. "Like Mack says—"

"Best for who? For what?" Fontenelli chimed in.

Every one began talking at once, and the briefing fell into total disarray. Bolan shouted them down and soon restored order. "Wait 'til you get all the facts," he told them. "Now listen to me. I assume that most of you came into the squad because of the money angle. That's just great with me, and I'm thankful to have had your services. But you have to know—these new pressures have altered the timetable and also the money potential. We've reached the showdown stage of the operation much quicker than I'd expected. All of a sudden the gravy has disappeared, and we're down to the raw meat of the situation. It's warfare now, pure and simple. What I'm saying is, the glory is gone from this operation. All that's left now is the hell. I want you to understand that. And I want to give you the chance to cash in your chips and get out of the game."

"What are *you* going to do?" Deadeye Washington inquired soberly.

Bolan showed him a grin. "Well . . . I'm in it for the hell. I'm going to finish the operation."

"By yourself?" Andromede asked.

"He's not by hisself," Washington said quickly, beating Bolan's reply. "Gravy always has been too rich all by itself. I'll take some of the hell, too."

"Hell yes," Gunsmoke Harrington spoke up. "I'm not splitting, Sarge."

"Well, talk it over between yourselves," Bolan said. "Politician will cash you out if you decide to leave. I'm going down to the beach. I'm recessing this briefing for half an hour. When I get back, we'll plan the grand slammer around what's left of the squad. Thanks and good luck to all of you,

126

leaving or staying." Bolan spun about and walked quickly toward the water.

"Well kiss my ass!" Fontenelli exclaimed quietly.

"It looks like at least three positive makes and two more possibles," Lieutenant Andy Foster reported to Captain Braddock. "The Indian, we're pretty certain, is Thomas Loudelk, a full-blooded Blackfoot from a reservation up in Montana. He knew Bolan in Vietnam. Disposed of his possessions last week and left the reservation. Tried to cash a thousand-dollar telegraphic money order there. Finally had to go into Butte to cash it. That money order was filed from the Western Union main office here in L.A. The sender was a B. Mackay."

Braddock grunted. "I'd say that's positive. Any line on him at this end?"

Foster shook his head. "Not a thing, but we're still working it. Here's another, a real colorful character they called Gunsmoke in Vietnam. He wore old-Western-style six-shooters, one on each hip. Just a kid, but they say the Viet cong were in real awe of the guy. He's been working out at the wild-West park since his discharge, one of those quick-draw artists. Walked off the job one day last week without notice." The lieutenant raised a meaningful gaze to his superior. "Told his boss he'd fired his last blank. Nice kid, they say. Easygoing, likable, good-looking—always had a bunch of girls clustered around him. Name's James Harrington. Father owns a sheep ranch up in Idaho. Hasn't shown up there, and the old man doesn't seem to care if he never does."

"Friend of Bolan's?"

Foster nodded. "Practically a disciple. He was living down in Anaheim. Moved out of his apartment the same day he quit his job. No forwarding address."

"Call it a positive," Braddock said. "Who's next?"

"Well ... that's Zitka. The telex from Saigon confirms the make. He was Bolan's right-hand man—sniping team, you know—for more than a year. They worked like a hand in a glove. Zitka was a forward member, the advance recon man. The Viets had a name for him that translates into English as Whispering Death. He's got almost as many decorations as Bolan."

"Let's look at those two possibles."

"This one here is Rosario Blancanales. Special-services sergeant, knew the country over there like a native. Doubles as a medic and an all-around handyman. Does a little bit of everything— mechanic, gunsmith, plays a couple of musical instruments. Organized schools for the village kids and even had a baseball little league going over there in unpacified territory. Say he has a genius for organization and administration. Twice he was recommended for OCS and twice he flunked the entrance exams. Just not enough formal education, it seems."

"How would he tie in with Bolan?"

He left special services after his second OCS failure, went into an elite combat unit. Worked with Bolan several times as a guide in enemy territory."

"And where is he now?" Braddock asked.

Foster sighed. "He's just a possible, remember. He was working at the VA hospital down in Long Beach. Gave notice that he was leaving long before Bolan came on the scene—about a month ago. His supervisor down there told our man that Blancanales was planning on reenlisting in the army. He left his job on schedule, right to the day of his notice, and he left no tracks at all. None. He didn't

128

reenlist anywhere in Southern California, I can tell you that."

"Doesn't seem to fit the pattern," Braddock mused.

"No, but he *has* disappeared, and he *did* disappear just after the gunfight out at Zitka's."

"All right. Keep checking. Who's the other possible?"

"Angelo Fontenelli, also known as Chopper. Heavy-weapons man over in Vietnam, another Bolan sidekick. He's married, has a wife and two kids in New Jersey. The wife claims she hasn't seen or heard of him for two years, and furthermore she's had no child support from him since his government checks stopped coming. That's how she knew he'd been discharged. Or so she says."

"What do you have to tie him to Bolan?"

"Nothing except the past association. In Vietnam. He's on the suspect list simply because we can't locate him."

"Okay. Keep on him. How're you doing with those vehicles?"

"Hell, that's damn near impossible, Tim, without some more info to go on."

"Yeah. Well . . . we got one lucky break. Lyons' detail turned up an electronics wholesaler who sold a sizable order of UHF radio equipment this morning. The buyer claimed to be from some technical school. Bought the stuff in loose lots. You know—chassis, components, crystals, odds and ends. Claimed the stuff would be used by students learning to build radio sets."

"Sounds reasonable," Lieutenant Foster commented.

"Sure, except the name he gave for the school doesn't check out, and he paid cash for the stuff. Several thousand dollars. What kind of school sends out a buyer with cash money in his jeans?"

"Smells like a hot buy, doesn't it?"

"Sure does. Lyons is down there now getting an itemized list of the sale.

Foster shifted awkwardly in his chair and asked, "What . . . uh, what's the latest on Rickert?"

"Stop, you're making me sick at my stomach," Braddock growled.

"You figure he got tipped?"

"Yeah, and I'd give a month's salary to learn how. Betty said he got a call while he was in the bullroom. Said he turned white as a ghost. He went back into the bullroom, told Menkes he had to personally investigate a hot tip, and he walked out. Five minutes before we went after him. That's the last anybody's seen of him. I don't—"

The ringing of the telephone on Braddock's desk interrupted his spiel. He scooped up the instrument and said, "Braddock." His eyes widened and focused owlishly on Foster. "Okay. Yeah. Keep on it and keep me informed. Yeah."

Braddock slowly cradled the phone. "It's starting to crack wide open," he told the lieutenant. "That was Granger. A car buyer down on Figueroa made a lot purchase from an individual today. The deal involved a red 1968 Corvette Stingray, and blue 1967 Ford Custom, a gray 1967 Mustang, and a 1963 Mercury station wagon."

"Bingo!" Foster exclaimed.

"Yeah, and listen, how lucky can you get? The name of the seller?"

"Yeah?"

"Rosario Blancanales! Except for the Corvette, the pink slips were all in his name, never reregistered. He'd only had the cars one week from the previous owners. Told the buyer he'd bought the cars for resale but his plans had gone sour and now he had to have his money back out of them.

130

The Corvette has Nevada registration and a bill of sale made out to one Bill Mackay."

"Now where does this leave us?" Foster asked, eyes narrowing speculatively.

"Leaves us a bit smarter," Braddock replied. "We can stop looking for those particular vehicles. We can move Blancanales into the positive-make column. And maybe . . . well, I wonder of Bolan is getting ready to blow town."

"Doesn't add up," Foster said. "Not if he's the one who bought the radio stuff."

"Let's assume that he is. So . . . he is not blowing town. He's shifting gears. He's dumped the hot vehicles, and he'll be picking up some more. Assume that he won't steal, he'll buy. Okay, let's—"

Carl Lyons stepped through the open doorway. The excitement in his manner stopped Braddock in midsentence. "What've you got, Carl?" Braddock inquired.

"It scares me, what I've got," Lyons declared. He advanced to Braddock's desk and placed a wrinkled sheet of onion-skin paper in front of the captain. "The list of radio parts. Look at those crystals, about halfway down the page."

"I'm looking. What am I looking for?"

"This is UHF, crystal-controlled stuff. Look at the frequencies he bought."

"I'm looking, Carl, but I still don't—"

"Dammit, Captain, he's covered our Hardcase frequencies!"

Braddock glared tight-lipped at the sheet of paper. Foster half-rose from his chair and craned about to get a look at the parts list.

"Well I'll be a . . ." Foster declared in a near whisper.

"How did that son of a bitch get our frequencies?" Lyons inquired angrily.

Braddock was woodenly shuffling through the

intelligence items Foster had placed on his desk earlier. He found the piece he was seeking and spread it out under the desklamp. It was a mug shot, the type of photo used on armed-forces identification cards, of a man with dark skin, thick black hair, and piercing eyes.

"Who is that?" Lyons asked.

"That," Captain Braddock said, "is an Indian. Not a Cherokee or a Navajo, but a Blackfoot. He was standing right there in my doorway earlier today, said he'd seen the Hollywood rhubarb last night. I sent him on down to the control room to file a written statement. I sent him in there myself."

Lyons could not control the sudden twitching at his facial muscles. "Those nervy bastards," he said, grinning. "What're you going to do with nervy bastards like that?"

"I'm going to lock them in a cell and throw away the key, that's what I'm going to do with them," Braddock said. He sighed, staring at the photo of Bloodbrother Loudelk. "It's almost a damn shame."

"And a waste," Foster added. "Think of what they could do, with those brains and energies, if they—"

"What *could* they do?" Lyons asked, quietly interrupting. "I mean, really, what could they do? They became men in a different sort of world—entirely different."

"They've got to live in this one, though," Braddock snapped. His manner clearly implied that the maudlin hour was over. He viciously punched a button on his intercom. "I want all Hardcase personnel on duty immediately. All detail leaders in the control room in thirty minutes. And get me some communications specialists up here right away. What's the latest on that electronics-intelligence outfit from San Diego?"

132

"The navy is flying them up from Miramer," came the response. "Should get here any minute now."

"With all their gear?"

"Yes, sir, with all their gear."

Braddock released the intercom button and pinned Lyons with a stern gaze. "That's what we're going to do with the nervy bastards," he told him. "We're going to beat them at their own game."

Julian DiGeorge did not like this Mack Bolan business, he did not like it at all. He wished there could have been some way to avoid this show-down, some way to be rid of the Bolan nuisance without going back to the old ways. When a man reaches the age of fifty-seven, "Deej" reasoned, he should be able to settle down in a peaceful enjoyment of the fruits of his lifetime of labor. Deej, of course, used the word "labor" in the loosest sense; he had no actual firsthand knowledge of what the term even implied. His father had been a gun-bearer in the early Capone era and had died in a federal prison. Little Deej had matriculated early into gangland circles, serving as a messenger and bag man on Chicago's South Side at the age of thirteen. There had been no labor involved in that occupation nor in the successive moves into num-bers, narcotics, prostitution, organized gambling, and finally into the family hierarchy. Labor, to Deej, meant carrying a gun. It meant police roust-ings and harassment and an occasional short "va-cation" behind bars; it meant worry and anxiety, competition with ambitious opportunists within the family, and living most of his days and nights under police suspicion and scrutiny.

Deej had not labored for quite a few years. He had been "Legit," to all outward appearances, throughout the sixties. He had backed nearly a dozen independently produced motion pictures. He owned three first-class nightclubs and was a behind-the-scenes force in many banking activities. More than one celebrity of stage and screen owed his start to the background maneuvering of this quiet patron of the arts. Understandably, Deej did not like this Mack Bolan business at all.

Many people nowadays, especially those in the upcoming generations, had never heard the words "Mafia" or "Costa Nostra." When they did, it was usually in some fairy-tale setting, a fiction, a legend. Deej himself laughed politely when the words were humorously employed by television or nightclub comics. So, understandably, Deej was highly upset with Mack Bolan. Thanks to Bolan, the words were now being heard everywhere a guy turned—and they weren't being used humorously. Already the President of the country was using this word in official documents sent to the congress. Yeah. Thanks to Bolan, Deej's peaceful enjoyment of a lifetime's fruits was being threatened. Thanks to Bolan, Deej was going to have to crawl from under that very comfortable "legit" cover, if only to make sure that it was still securely in place.

There were still many facets of the DiGeorge activities that Deej did not want to see exposed to the public eye. The import business down at the Port of Los Angeles, for instance, and its warehouses bulging with untaxed commodities. The SS *Pacific Palace*, for instance, with its girls and gaming tables. His partial interest in Tri-Coast, for instance, and their recent exposure as a Mafia money drop. There were many vital business and political connections, also, that would be severed for Deej under the Bolan spotlight.

Deej had tried to evade the Bolan showdown. He had offered to put up another hundred thou out of his own pocket to strengthen the open contract on Bolan. He had even suggested that perhaps Bolan could be bought off, perhaps even brought into the family with a full pardon for his sins. But Deej knew, from the wisdom of a lifetime of "labor," that he'd just been trying to postpone the inevitable. Bolan would have to be met and squashed. There was no evading the showdown. The guy had a hard-on for the family—it was that simple. They'd have to castrate him; they could not screw him to death or sate him with games of romance. There was only one way to castrate a guy with that big a hard-on. You had to go back to the old ways. You had to get a gun and shove it down his throat and pull the trigger.

Julian "Deej" DiGeorge would have to become a laborer again, briefly. He had already sent his wife and his daughter and his grandchildren to Palm Springs for a quiet vacation. Now Deej would return to the salt mines for a little while. Deej had no choice. He was the big uncle of Southern California. And tonight, the family was coming to council. It would be a death council. For Bolan's death.

Chapter Thirteen

THE COUNCIL

The Death Squad was waiting for Bolan when he returned from his solitary stroll along the beach. None had left; all were present. Bolan gave no outward sign of pleasure at this development, but his voice was warm and his eyes were sparkling as he said, "All right, let's get on with the briefing."

He produced a stack of Polaroid snapshots, which he handed to Zitka. "Everyone take a good look at these. Pass them around. Brother and I were on site a little while ago, and we tried to cover every angle. Study them carefully. We'll be going in under cover of darkness; I want you to have a good idea of the lay of the land.

"The front of the house faces west, away from the street, looking down on a gentle slope. The patio is flagstoned, runs about a hundred feet deep, seventy-five feet wide, on the upper level and is accessible from the ground floor of the house through these French doors, set into a cement-block wall. The other wall, down at the end of the patio, is only about two feet high. Beyond the wall is terraced lawn—not as steep as it looks in these pictures—three levels. The swimming pool is on the first level below the patio. The tennis court is at the south side of the house. Bocci-ball and putting greens on the north side. The driveway, from the street to the parking area at the rear of the house, is about 200 yards. The terrain is slightly uneven but generally level. There are flower gardens and a number of small ponds back there.

"The only fence is up here along the street. It's

136

hurricane fencing, eight feet high, and ends at the hedges at either side. The stone gateway stands open; there isn't even a gate. It's wide enough to take two cars. The hedges running along the north and south boundaries look very thick—and they are, except right along the ground. It should be easy enough to penetrate, if we decide to go that route. This is not a 'hard' house. It is soft, very soft, entirely vulnerable, easily reached and breached. DiGeorge obviously feels secure and respectable enough to have not bothered with fortifications."

Bolan paused to light a cigarette. "For that very reason," he continued, exhaling as he spoke, "I have an idea that his troops might break and run when the shooting starts. If they do, we'll give hot chase. They just might lead us to their 'hard' house. I feel certain they have one, somewhere in the area."

Zitka spoke up. "You get any feeling for the interior layout of the house?"

Bolan wagged his head. "No, and I doubt that we'll need it. The way it looked to Brother and me, they're going to hold their council outside, on the patio. They were setting up the bars and stocking them when we were out there."

"Italianos like a bit of beef and beverage with their business meetings," Andromede commented with a smile.

Fontenelli shifted about restlessly. "I been wondering when the Italiano bit would start," he muttered.

"Hell, I didn't mean anything like that," Andromede replied quickly. "Some of my best friends are Italianos."

Deadeye Washington guffawed loudly. "Where've I heard that line before?" he howled.

137

"Sometimes I wonder if I'm on the wrong side," Fontenelli grumbled.

"Okay, knock it off," Bolan commanded in a mild voice. "This's no race war, and it sure as hell is no vendetta against the Italian people."

"What the hell you think the Mafia is?" Andromede said, grinning.

"It's Dago Power, man," Washington said gleefully.

Everyone except Fontenelli laughed. "*Mafia* don't mean the same thing as *Italian*," he said stiffly. "Who the hell you think was catching all the hell from the Maffianos back inna old days, back inna old country? Italianos got no love for those bastards. I never even *knew* anybody in the Mafia, in my whole life."

"Hey, kid, cool it," Andromede said. "We're just having fun."

"I got a better reason than anybody here to hate them bastards," Fontenelli persisted. "They give the whole Italian race a bad name."

"Shit, I love the goddamn Italianos!" Andromede declared emotionally. "Especially the women! Oooo, them goddamn lovin' women! Didn't I tell you I was going back to Jersey with you someday? Didn't I?"

"Okay, so I'm oversensitive," Fontenelli said grudgingly. He glanced at Washington and smiled.

Washington winked at him. "They let black people in that Mafia?"

Fontenelli chuckled. "Well, they used to call it The Black Hand."

"Oooo-*eee!* They gonna have to integrate *all* of me, man, not just my black hands."

Bolan was glad for the brief personal exchange. It had released some tensions. But time was growing short. "Okay, back to the war," he said. "And back to Zitter's question. I doubt that we'll need to worry about the interior of DiGeorge's house. If they retreat into the house, we will not go in after them. We'll just strafe hell out of it and then abort the mission. Can't take the risk of trying to smoke them out, because the cops will be on the scene damn quick—I feel sure of that. So—"

Gunsmoke Harrington said, "You're basing our strategy, then, on them breaking and running right after we make contact."

Bolan nodded. "Or soon after. There's a . . . well, here's my reasoning. The word is out, see. These people know that the police are planning a rousting operation, to begin tomorrow morning. Now. What's the purpose of this council tonight? First, I figure, is to set the strategy for a counteroffensive against us. The second item of business will undoubtedly have to do with the police threat. I just can't believe that they will want to go on home and wait for the cops to begin the harassment. A lot of these people are living highly respectable roles, and they don't like their names in the police news any more than any other respectable citizen would.

"So here's what I think they'll decide to do. I think they will decide to join forces against us. I think they will decide to leave home for a while. The best possible place for them to achieve both objectives at the same time is at their hard site. I know damn well they have one somewhere in the area. In three different recorded conversations today, Varone mentioned 'the family home.' They have one—and we want to help them decide to go there. Okay?"

"Sounds reasonable." Zitka commented.

"Okay." Bolan stepped over to a portable blackboard, on which was drawn a rough sketch of the DiGeorge neighborhood. "First I want to set the positions. Then we'll run through the individual

139

missions. Deadeye and I will be on this hillside to the west, with the long pieces. Bloodbrother is above us, on the rim of the hill, eagling. Chopper and Gunsmoke at the rear, here . . . and here . . . flanking with the automatics. Zitter and Boom on tracking stations, here . . . and here . . . I may have to call you in if things go sour, so be ready for a fire mission. Flower Child on the south flank, rear. Get your grenade launcher, Flower, and stake out a good spot to fly from."

Andromede grinned and wet his lips.

"Chopper will cover you when you begin your grenade assault. Now—Gadgets will be inside the horse, Politician driving. Keep that big mother moving, Pol, and don't get in too close. Gadgets will be monitoring the police radio nets and keeping us posted on their activities. I want every man in radio harness and his ears open. This could be—"

"I've been doing some thinking about this," Gadgets Schwarz said, interrupting Bolan. "And I'm worried."

"What's worrying you, Gadgets?"

"I've been wondering if these cops have the ability to ECM us. If they do, that van could become a Trojan horse in reverse."

"What is ECM?"

"Electronic counter measures. Electronic spying, in other words. Like on our spy ships and spy planes. Remember the *Pueblo*? Well—"

"Are you talking about radar?" Zitka asked. "How the hell could radar do them any good in a crowded area like this?"

"Naw, hell," Schwarz said disgustedly. "I mean—"

"Radio direction finders." Bolan muttered.

Schwarz nodded. "Yeah, the same principle, only they got some mighty damn sophisticated

140

stuff out now. They can scan-through and lock onto another transmitter in nothing flat."

"How do they do that," Bolan asked musingly, "if they don't know what frequencies are being transmitted on?"

"I said they scan-through," Schwarz replied. "They don't need to know your frequency. They *find* your frequency with a scanner. Then, just like a computer, they lock on a couple of peripheral stations and get an automatic triangulation on you."

"Suppose you're moving? Damn fast?"

"Then they ECM you every time you transmit, and they track you. They plot a course, speed, the whole bit. Just like radar from that point on, except they're depending on your transmissions to trigger their equipment."

"It's pretty sophisticated stuff, Gadgets?"

"Yeah. *Damn* sophisticated. I don't guess these cops would have anything like that. Wouldn't have that much use for it."

"Suppose they did," Bolan said. "Could we counteract it?"

Schwarz shook his head. "Not with the stuff we have. Our only defense would be to keep quiet as much as possible. Keep transmissions brief."

"How brief?"

"Three or four seconds at a time. That brief."

"All right," Bolan said. "We'll play it that way. The radios will be used only when absolutely necessary. We will not acknowledge each other's transmissions. Rely on code words as much as possible. Don't say anything that may give away your position or route. Okay." Bolan had drawn on a troubled frown. "I want every man in nightsuits, blackface, and as light as possible. You flankers will provide covering and diverting fire only. Trackers, I want you to . . ."

The man of the squad listened in silence to the balance of the full-scale combat briefing, interrupting only to quietly request a clarification of some detail, each one clearly realizing the importance of a complete understanding. Each man present was fully aware that this was a rehearsal for the death game.

"Listen, you get plenty of boys out in the open," DiGeorge instructed Zeno Varone. "I want them everywhere, all over the place. Out front, out back, on the street, I want 'em swarming all over the place. If that guy is keeping tabs on us, I don't want him getting any ideas to make a hit on *this* place."

"You think he's watching us, Deej?" Varone inquired solemnly.

"If he's as smart as they say—sure, he's watching us." DiGeorge stepped to the edge of the patio and gazed off toward the distant hillside, darkly skylined against the starry night. "Maybe from up there someplace, if he's all that smart. With a good pair of binoculars, he could look down my kitchen sink."

"Maybe he'd hit us from over there," Varone observed nervously.

"Hey," DiGeorge scoffed, "if he's that good, we don't need to kill 'im, we need to convert 'im. Eh? Don't be an old maid, Zeno. Don't go looking under your bed and in your closet every night, eh? This Bolan is just a guy, like any other guy. He thinks he's hell on wheels, though—a boy commando or something. When he hits, he hits with thunder and lightning. Eh? Look at the way he handled 'Milio. Both times, eh? Thunder and lightning, eh? He can't do anything like that from a half a mile away."

142

"I guess not, Deej." Varone was still gazing nervously toward the hills.

"So get the boys out where he can see them, in case he's curious. I don't want no thunder and lightning around here. I don't need that kind of publicity."

"Leonardo's arrived," Varone said, looking toward the house.

"Yeah, okay, take his boys too. Make sure they understand, I *want* them to be seen. It's about time to start. Go on, now, get those boys spread around."

Varone jerked his head in an obedient nod and set off quickly toward the house. DiGeorge walked slowly along the edge of the patio, his eyes absently searching the darkness at the fringe of the lighted area. He chuckled to himself and decided that he should listen to his own advice. This guy Bolan would not be so dumb as to try a hit here tonight. He wondered, though. He wondered just how many thunder-and-lightning tricks this guy had up his sleeve. Then he saw that the nephews were taking their places at the big table at the center of the patio. He pushed the boy commando out of his thoughts for the moment, fixed a big grin on his face, and strode commandingly to the council table.

Deadeye Washington was lying prone in a shallow trough, a clump of umbrella trees to his rear, the long rifle supported by a small tripod. His right eye was fastened to the eyepiece of the large sniperscope, and he was smiling. Just to his left was Mack Bolan, like a twin, sighting down through the big twenty power and grinning.

"Wish I could read lips." Bolan grunted.

"Yeah, man, that'd be cool," Washington agreed

143

quietly. "That's Varone there on the right, the little guy. You figure white-hair is the big daddy?"

"Probably. Looks the part. We'll know for sure when they take their places at the table."

"You're pretty sure about the range?"

Bolan grunted. "Double check me, Deadeye. See the back wall of the house? Those cement blocks measure about eight inches from seam to seam, so . . . let's say the top of the seventh block should be five feet off the ground."

"Yeah." Deadeye emitted a long, hissing sigh, then said, "Okay, I get a scale of . . ." He pulled his eye off the scope and craned back to peer at a card that had been taped to the stock of the rifle. "You're right, 600 meters is the range." Deadeye sighed again and returned his eye to the scope. "Man, that's a long ways off."

"Figure about one second for these Magnums to make the trip," Bolan advised.

"Yeah. A scared man could travel halfway across that patio in that time. I got quite an oversight, too, even with these Magnums. Your piece sighted in a little bit better than mine. I gotta hold over twenty inches at this range."

"Not exactly fish in a barrel, is it?" Bolan said. "Uh . . . what do you figure for the length of that table, Deadeye?"

"Oh . . . I'd say . . . fifteen feet. Hey! There's a lotta people movin' around down there now. Where'd white-hair go to?"

"Head of the table, to your right. He's your big daddy, all right. Hand me those glasses, Deadeye. Field of vision through this scope is . . ."

"Like lookin' through a microscope," Deadeye finished. He passed the binoculars over without disturbing his own position at the rifle.

Bolan took the glasses and raised up over his rifle. "That's better," he said, surveying the

144

DiGeorge layout in the larger field afforded by the binoculars. "And you're right. They're moving the troops around. Plain sight. Now what the hell . . . ?"

"How many d'you make, Sarge?"

Bolan was moving the glasses in a slow sweep of the expansive grounds. "Hell, about a full company in full sight," he replied slowly. "And they're turning lights on all around."

"Maybe they've flipped. Combat fatigue."

Bolan chuckled. "No. No . . . I think . . . maybe it's meant to be a show of strength."

"Oh. Like a peacock raisin' its tail, huh?"

"Yeah," Bolan replied, grinning. He swiveled his head toward his left shoulder, depressed the transmitter button, and said, "Horse. Anything?"

Five seconds passed; then Schwarz's voice replied, "Negative. Clear."

Bolan counted to ten, then punched the button again. "Flower." (Pause.) "Take Able Four." (Pause.) "Launch five on signal." (Pause.) "Chopper, cover. Out."

"That'll make Flower very happy," Washington commented softly. "That man sure loves that little grenade launcher."

Bolan nodded grimly and again addressed the radio transmitter. "Caution, caution." He waited ten seconds; then: "Company strength. Extreme caution."

"You're not giving them cops much to zot on to," Washington said, grinning broadly.

Bolan smiled at Washington and fitted his eye to the scope. "Gadgets shook me up," he admitted. "I don't want to take anything for granted, not where these L.A. cops are concerned. I don't give them one damn advantage."

"Those people down there sure giving *us* one,"

Washington observed. "Even got the table turned our way."

Bolan's heavy rifle was swiveling in its tripod as he slowly tracked along the faces at the council table. "Remember—one second to impact," he reminded his partner. "The man to DiGeorge's left, first one, the fat one, with his back to you. Got him in your field?"

"Yeah, I got him. Don't like the looks of those chairs, though. I'd like to take 'im above the shoulders."

"Any way you want, Deadeye. He's yours. After the scramble, it's sniper's choice. I'm taking the guy to DiGeorge's right."

"What are you holding on for your correction?"

"I'm using the top of the glass door in the background."

Washington sniffed. "Okay. I'll take about an inch offa that. What do you figure for wind?"

"Let's call it a dead calm."

"Dead is right," Washington said. "I'm ready, if you wanta start the count."

"On *five*," Bolan replied. He took a deep breath and began releasing it in short bursts as he counted, his finger tightening slowly on the hair trigger. "One . . . two . . . three . . ."

Chapter Fourteen

BEVERLY HELL

Flower Child Andromede reached into the trunk of the automobile and hastily unwrapped the felt-covered grenade launcher, affixed it to his rifle, and snatched up a prepared pouch of rifle grenades. Then he slammed the trunk door and jogged around the end of the car and ran along a six-foot-high wall that fronted the property directly adjacent to the DiGeorge estate. About fifty feet before reaching the thick hedgerow that marked DiGeorge's line, Andromede vaulted to the top of the wall and slithered along on his belly for another twenty feet, halting in the protective overhang of a date-palm frond.

He could see the rear of the DiGeorge house clearly from this position and could even hear small groups of men moving noisily about the grounds, laughing and passing wisecracks back and forth. The entire place was brightly lighted. Two men were playing toss with a tennis ball beneath the floodlights of the tennis court. Another group was at the opposite side of the yard, rolling small balls along a luxuriously green runway. Bolan had been right, and then some. Andromede could spot a full company on this end of the estate alone. He smiled and fitted a grenade onto the launcher. It was going to be "liberation night" for quite a few earthbound entities.

Andromede, however, did not feel quite ready for liberation himself. He carefully calculated an assault pattern to provide him the best possible chance for a successful withdrawal, arranged his grenades along the wall for a quick pickup-and-reload capability, then quietly awaited the signal. He was vaguely wondering where Chopper was, when a thick shadow detached itself from the hedges just forward of his position. He immediately recognized the squat bulk of Fontenelli and softly cleared his throat to signal his position. Fontenelli moved into the shadow of the wall and advanced silently, to stand just beneath him.

"You see okay from up there?" Fontenelli hissed.

"Perfect," Andromede whispered. "I'm going to walk 'im in from right to left, up by the house. That oughta jar the piss out of 'em."

"Hope Bolan knows what he's doing," Fontenelli said after a brief silence. "That joint is crawling alive with some of the meanest hoods in the country."

"Better keep it quiet," Andromede suggested. "Four of them were walking along the hedge there a couple of minutes ago."

"I wanta tell you somethin'," Fontenelli hissed.

"Make it quick."

"You know 'bout my old lady and her screwin' around while I was in 'Nam."

"Yeah, I know."

"We got two kids back in Jersey."

"Yeah, I know."

"If I don't make it, I want my bucks to go to my kids. To the *kids*, not to Miss Hotpants."

"You'll make it, Chopper."

"Yeah, but if I don't . . ."

"Okay, don't worry—I'll take care of it."

"Maybe you won't make it either. Tell Bolan, on the radio."

"Tell him yourself."

"Can't. I lost it."

"You lost your *radio*?"

"Yeah. Somewhere back there in those hedges. Damn harness came loose."

"Stay close to me then."

"Yeah. Tell Bolan, eh?"

"Okay. Now shut up."

Fontenelli moved silently away. Andromedē watched him drop to the ground and crawl into the hedges; then he lost sight of him. Chopper's concern had momentarily unnerved the young Puerto Rican. What the hell—they were all fully aware of the chances. That was the name of the game, wasn't it? Live until liberation. Liberate the other guy before he can liberate you. That was the game. Andromede shivered involuntarily. He was not yet quite ready to end the game, despite all his bravado concerning life and death. Liberation was much easier to contemplate when it was happening to the other guy. Andromede cleared his mind of the unessentials, kept his ears open for the signal from Bolan, and cast his contemplations toward the liberation of others.

Then a distant, double cra-*aack* of twin high-powered rifles firing simultaneously split the calm and froze Andromede's contemplations. Someone at the far side of the house was yelling. The cra-*aacks* were coming in rapid succession now, and men were running about excitedly in the yard next door, cursing loudly and calling to one another.

Andromede smiled grimly and tensed at the trigger, his ear bent to the small radio. The liberation was on.

Julian DiGeorgē did not like the attitudes of some of his nephews. Some of them seemed more worried about their standing in the community than about the threat to the family. And it seemed that everybody wanted to talk about the forthcoming police roustings more than they wanted to plan for the already established threat to Mack Bolan. Leonardo Cacci, the smooth, college-educated

149

nephew at DiGeorge's right hand, was on the board of three banks, he was coming up big in local politics, and he was very unhappy with the thought of taking up a gun and taking on a fight that was obviously so far beneath his personal image.

Cacci's ivory smile might charm the female voters of his congressional district, but it sometimes made DiGeorge want to throw up. DiGeorge's underworld earnings had provided the money that built the braces that had kept the ivory in that smile. Cacci was a nephew; it was one thing to put on legit airs in public, quite another to try to snow Uncle Deej with "one's" responsibility to "one's" community. DiGeorge wondered just how far Leonardo would survive without the constant propping of family money. "One" would not survive far, that was certain.

Then there was Johnny Trieste. Yes, there was always Johnny Trieste, it seemed. He sat at DiGeorge's left, a great, hulking pig of a man who had never found it possible to become a "one." Johnny had been around for as long as DiGeorge could remember, and he'd never changed one hair, not one fat wrinkle. He spoke English with the overtone accent of a nightclub comic, and he had never learned to read it or to write it—but he could count American bucks. Yes, he could certainly count American bucks.

Johnny had never been anything more than a bagman, but he'd been the best bagman in the business. And nobody could complain about a man who'd become the best at anything—if that was all he wanted to do. But Johnny was sort of embarrassing, at times, to be around. He did not blend into the new environment, the new circles—he did not even blend into the family any more. He had been a loyal Maffiano, though, loyal to the very core.

150

And he'd been around long enough that he had a certain influence in the family councils. Right now, Johnny Trieste was terribly concerned over the possible police harassment. Johnny had been dodging a murder conviction for thirty years. He had made a courtroom escape in New York just moments before the reading of the death sentence and had made his way west and enjoyed the protection of the family all these years. Still, each potential contact with the police sent him into tremors. DiGeorge felt a sympathy for the old Maffiano, but . . . business was business, and the family came first.

Johnny Trieste was hunched over the table, staring into a glass of wine, and Leonardo Cacci was regarding him with one of those phony ivory smiles. DiGeorge was saying, "Look—first things first, Let's talk about—"

And then something had happened to the back of Johnny's head; it seemed to just burst open for no apparent reason. At that exact moment, Leonardo's smile disappeared in a shower of ivory and frothy blood. For a startled instant, DiGeorge thought that Johnny's shattered head had flown over into Leonardo's mouth. Johnny's huge bulk settled onto the table in a way that left no doubt in DiGeorge's mind that the thirty-year-old death sentence had finally been executed. Leonardo's head had jerked back suddenly, the body following and rocking the chair onto its rear legs; then over he went, chair and all. Only then did the twin cra-*aacks* announce the reason behind it all.

All others sat frozen in the immediate reaction to the inexplicable behavior of Cacci and Trieste; then two more at the table were flung violently about, even as the initial gunfire reports reached the assembled ears.

DiGeorge let out a loud yell and found that

151

long-dormant instincts were still strong enough to propel him into a wild sideways fling toward the floor. The distant soundings of the high-powered rifles continued incessantly, and men and bodies were flying about in all directions.

"Turnitover turnitover! Turn the goddamn table over!" DiGeorge screamed, scrabbling desperately at the leg of the heavy oaken piece. The table crashed to the flagstones. DiGeorge scrambled behind it on his belly, one edge of his reeling consciousness aware of the litter of bodies behind him, another edge taking note of other men running in all directions. He saw two of them lurch suddenly as though stricken by some sudden paralysis, then crash to the ground.

"Good, God, good God, it's a slaughter," he moaned, his breath moving painfully through a constricted rib cage. Thunder and lightning, indeed, had found their way to Julian DiGeorge. And he had only the faintest idea whence it came.

"That's right, baby, run straight," Deadeye Washington muttered. He squeezed the hair trigger and was already swinging toward a new target before the thundering convulsion of the big gun had spent itself against his shoulder.

"Okay—evaluation!" Bolan snapped, speaking even as his partner's weapon thundered again.

When Washington hoisted himself off the eyepiece, Bolan was sitting upright, legs folded, holding the binoculars to his eyes with one hand and massaging his shoulder with the other.

"Damn thing jars hell out of you," Bolan muttered.

"Yeah. What're they doing down there now?"

"Flopping about like headless chickens. Some are starting to look our way now. Give 'em a couple more rounds, Deadeye. See if they can spot your flashes."

Washington grinned and bent once again to his eyepiece. He fired two quick rounds into the heavy glass at the front of the house. Bolan, peering through the binoculars, smiled. "Believe you dropped about ten with that burst," he said.

"I just shot out the window," Washington replied, chuckling.

"And brought on ten heart attacks," Bolan said, chuckling along with him. He sobered abruptly, then smiled. "Yeah, they saw us. Here comes a guy with a Thompson, running hell bent for election. They're running for the lower wall." Bolan's smile grew. "Are they actually going to return our fire?"

A popping and crackling arose from the distant estate. Washington turned to Bolan with a broad grin and said, "Shi-iit."

Bolan tossed the glasses to Washington. "Now watch the fun," he told him. He thumbed the button on his transmitter and said, "Now, Flower, *go!*"

A loud, faraway blast echoed Bolan's words. He grinned at Washington. "Damn, he was primed, wasn't he? What's the reaction?"

Another blast sounded. "They were all running up from the rear," Washington reported. "Now they're standing and gawking at each other. Now they're starting back, but slow—*damn* slow."

"Let's keep them see-sawing," Bolan said. He was making good use of the rifle as he spoke. The grenade blasts were coming at ten-second intervals. The DiGeorge grounds were in pandemonium, flames sprouting up here and there, puffs of smoke drifting aimlessly about, men running everywhere. Bolan squeezed off calculated shots down the long range, and Washington joined in.

Minutes later, the heat from Bolan's rifle was becoming decidedly uncomfortable for the flesh of his face. Deadeye Washington stopped firing and pushed himself away. "This is worse than 'Nam. This is just jail. I lost my stomach for it, Mack."

Bolan raised off the hot rifle, his face set in grim lines. "The mighty Mafia," he intoned soberly. "Okay, Deadeye. Break the pieces down. It's time to get out of here." He spoke into the radio. "Horse. What's up?"

"Nothing," came the immediate response. "One call on the general net and then nothing. It smells. Hardcase is silent."

"*Break off!*" Bolan snarled. "Stand by to track!"

"God damn!" Schwarz cried. "I been ECMed!"

"How do you know?"

"I just know."

"Get rolling out of there!" Bolan commanded. "Move it! All units, break away and forget the track!"

"Negative," came Zitka's cool tones. "I'm on one and I'm sticking."

"Blue movement, coming up south," Loudelk's calm whisper announced.

Washington had the rifles in his arms. His eyes were flaring with excitement. Bolan jerked his head toward the crest of the hill, and his partner moved out immediately.

"More blues, coming west," Loudelk said, "and I'm breaking."

Bolan was sprinting up the slope behind Washington. Zitka's voice was coming through the small speaker. "Route Three, it's a line-up. This's paydirt. Suggest break and re-form on me."

"All who can," Bolan added. "But evade blues at all cost."

"I can't find Chopper," Andromede declared woefully.

"Break, Flower! Get the hell out!" Bolan had

154

reached the road and was transmitting as he ran for his vehicle.

"Chopper doesn't have a radio. He don't have the word!"

"Get . . . the . . . hell . . . *out!*"

"Goddammit, goddammit."

DiGeorge had made a hasty and careful check of the dead. Eight of the family had fallen, and there was unbelievable carnage among the hired hands. Only four of the twelve nephews who had come to the council survived, and still the raining bullets were richocheting off the flagstones, tearing through the table and slamming into the cement blocks of the back wall. And now a new note had been added—the explosions and the chattering of machine guns out back.

"Get out of here!" DiGeorge screamed. The four survivors of the ruling council turned frightened eyes onto him. "Through the house! Call your boys and blow! You hear? *Blow!*"

"Where we gonna go, Deej?" Zeno Varone whined.

"Get to Balboa! I'll meet you. But *get going!* Through the house!"

Varone nodded meekly and dragged himself across the flagstones. He had been nicked in the arm and was bleeding. The others quickly followed after him. "Now get to Balboa!" DiGeorge shouted. "And dig in, dammit, as soon as you get there!" He waited until they had cleared the patio; then he scrambled to his feet and zigzagged in a low crouch to the protection of the cement wall. He stepped through the shattered glass window and ran toward the rear of the house, colliding with his personal bodyguard, Lou Pena, in the kitchen. "What're you doin' in here?" DiGeorge snarled.

"There's a nut walkin' around out there with a

155

machine gun," Pena declared breathlessly. "I come in ta get the lights."

DiGeorge snatched the pistol from Pena's hand, pushed him aside, and stepped out the back door, then dropped to a crouch and made a run for the garage. When he was halfway there, all the lights went out. DiGeorge swore under his breath, then flung himself to the ground as a machine gun began chattering nearby. A cloud of smoke was drifting toward him; from out of the cloud stepped a squat figure wearing a black outfit and carrying a spitting machine gun. DiGeorge raised Pena's revolver and fired three rapid shots. The guy slumped to his knees without a sound, still holding the big gun. It continued to spit sporadic flame, but now it just chewed up the ground. The gunner was trying to bring the muzzle up, but it kept dropping lower and lower until it was resting on the ground. It ceased its chatter, and the guy dropped back onto his butt, then slumped forward.

DiGeorge scrambled to his feet and resumed his trip to the garage. He cast a quick glance over his shoulder. The guy in the black suit was still sitting there, a shadowy blob in the darkness, still trying to pull the gun out of the dirt.

DiGeorge tugged frantically at the garage door. There was no telling how many more guys like that one were wandering around his grounds. Beverly Hills had ceased to be a safe place for Julian DiGeorge. There was a better place. He had to get there—and the sooner the better.

Andromede had fired his first grenade even before Bolan's signal had been completed, and he was reaching for his third reload when he heard Chopper's chattergun go into action. Groups of Maffianos were racing madly about the DiGeorge grounds, shouting curses and instructions. One of them had yelled, *"On the wall!"*—and that was when Chopper cut loose.

Andromede could see the steady muzzle flashes licking out from Chopper's weapon, and the screams and shouts that immediately arose beyond the hedges told of his effect. The Puerto Rican had just fired his fifth round, when he saw that Chopper's muzzle flashes were now beyond the hedges and advancing.

Andromede screamed, "Chopper! Get back! *Chopper!*"—knowing, even as he did so, that his voice was lost in the explosive confusion of the Di-George grounds. He loaded his sixth grenade, leaped to his feet, and ran to the end of the wall. He had Chopper in sight now. The squat Italian was walking slowly but steadily across the grounds, firing from the chest in short bursts and scattering the enemy in a panicky retreat. Andromede could count about twelve men running toward the large house, their backs to Fontenelli—in full flight. He raised his grenadier, sighted beyond the heads of the fleeing enemy, and let it fly. The flame and smoke of the explosion momentarily obscured the landscape directly in front of Fontenelli. He halted and turned back toward Andromede.

"Get back!" Andromede shouted, rising to his toes and frantically waving an arm.

Fontenelli sent a figure-eight burst in Andromede's general direction, then spun about and disappeared into the smoke. Andromede slung his weapon and launched himself into the air. He cleared the hedge and hit the soft ground of the DiGeorge estate with a jarring impact just as all the lights flashed off. He paused to get his bearings, then had just stepped off in the direction Fontenelli had taken, when his radio came alive. He continued a cautious advance and listened to the exchange between Bolan and Schwarz, then stopped stock still at Bolan's "Break off" command. All was silent about him. A vehicle was gunning down the curving driveway, heading out in a squeal of tires. A muted burst of fire that sounded much like Chopper's weapon sounded from the smoky darkness ahead. He moved on, calling out softly for his partner.

"Evade Blues at all cost," Bolan's voice was telling him.

He punched his transmitter button and cried, "I can't find Chopper!"

"Break, Flower! Get the hell out!" Bolan commanded sharply.

"Chopper doesn't have a radio. He don't have the word!" Andromede protested.

"Get . . . the . . . hell . . . *out!*"

"Goddammit, goddammit," he said despairingly, then released the transmission switch and yelled, "Chopper! Break off, dammit. *Regroup!*"

A string of vehicles was whining along the drive now. Andromede wavered, then ran into the smoke.

He found Fontenelli seated on the ground about halfway between the street and the house. He was slumped forward and leaning on his weapon, the muzzle of which was dug into the turf. The front of his nightsuit was warmly wet and sticky, and his eyes stared unseeingly toward the ground. Andromede's quickly exploring fingers found three chest punctures. He laid his friend down alongside his weapon, closed the glazed eyes, and quickly walked away.

Chapter Fifteen

GRAND SLAM

The Porsche was careening down the hill, Washington behind the wheel, Bolan leaning against the opposite door with the radio in his hand.

"That's Bloodbrother, dead ahead," Washington pointed out.

Bolan jerked his head in a nod. "Stay on him," he said; then he spoke into the radio. "Horse! Dump and bail out! You have no chance in that jobby!"

"We got a better idea," Blancanales' voice reported. "We're gonna try a D and D."

"Negative," Bolan snapped. "Jump ship! Let it go!"

"Sorry, Sarge. It's a D and D. Our decision."

"What he talking about?" Washington asked, rolling his eyes toward Bolan. He quickly swung his attention back to his driving chores as the Porsche leaned into a sweeping ninety-degree turn.

"Dummy and Divert," Bolan muttered. "They're trying to lead off the blues."

"Think they can do it?"

Bolan sighed. "I don't know. They're gonna get themselves racked out, that's what. Just might swing the track from everyone else, though." He spoke again into the radio. "Where away, Horse?"

"Route Two and leveling. Gadgets found their new web. Stand by for intel."

"Route Three is maintaining," Zitka advised. Then: "Uh-oh. Trouble at the crossroads."

"What is it, Zit?"

159

"Roadblock! Damn—lookit that! They're running it!"

"*Break!*"

A brief silence; then: "It's Route Three, Junction Two. I am avoiding, resuming track beyond."

Bolan swore under his breath. Washington chuckled and sent the sports car into another squealing turn. "You said tonight's the night, and that's the last thing anyone believed," he told Bolan.

The voice of Gadgets Schwarz came through the radio, speaking in a rapid monotone. "Okay, here's the lay. Containment around periphery. Looks like a hole on Route Four, though. All exits at Routes Two and Three are sealed. Avoid. Run wide on Four. Out."

"Okay, that's great!" Bolan snapped into the radio. "Now, dammit, *bail!*"

"Negit," Schwarz replied. "D and D is bearing fruit. Will exercise options."

"Roll call!" Bolan commanded.

"Eagle is out and splitting wide on Four," from Bloodbrother Loudelk.

"Track's back on and streaking for skinnytail," said Zitka.

"Comin' 'round the mountain and closing," reported Boom-Boom Hoffower.

"Angling and running for Four," Gunsmoke Harrington sighed.

"I've got Horse in sight," said Flower Child Andromede. "Will cover all possible."

A brief silence followed. Bolan glanced at Washington, punched the transmitter, and barked, "Chopper! Where away?"

"He's away in a lay on the Beverly clay," Andromede reported in a flat voice. "He says spend his pension on the kids in Jersey."

"*Confirm!*" Bolan snarled.

"He's free, brother, and that's as confirmed as he's going to get."

"Run careful, dammit," Bolan muttered into the radio. "The price has already got too high."

Captain Braddock smacked a fist into an open palm and cried, "Get that hole plugged on the Golden State. That's the Route Four they're yakking about!"

The dispatcher waved an excited hand at Braddock and said, "Another gunfight. Pacific Coast and Beverly! The roadblock. Two more cars damaged. I got no nearby units to replace 'em."

Braddock lunged toward the console and quickly surveyed the map set into the glassed top of the desk. "Send these over," he instructed, his index finger circling a flagged area. He moved over to stand in front of an intercom. "Andy, what's the word up there?"

Lieutenant Andy Foster, on the roof with the special intelligence team from the U.S. Navy, responded immediately. "They're scattering like the pieces from an explosion. They've located the new Hardcase net, too, you know."

"Yeah, dammit, I know. I've been listening. What's that stuff about a horse?"

"A rolling control center, we gather. Probably the van."

"Stay on them. Let me know when a definite route of travel can be established." Braddock sighed and turned back to the dispatcher. "Let's swirl south," he said. "Start 'em moving."

"They don't even know what they're looking for, Captain," the dispatcher replied in a low voice.

"Dammit, I know that. But get 'em moving anyway."

The dispatcher nodded and turned back to his

console. "Zone Four," he announced, "Zone Five, Zone Six—all units, commence . . ."

Braddock turned away with a heavy frown and walked toward the coffee service. It was happening, the thing he'd feared most. The drag that had been activated for Bolan was engaging the fleeing Mafia vehicles first—and blood was flowing in L.A. streets. The captain sighed and half-filled his cup with coffee. He knew, somehow, that tonight was to be the climax to the Bolan affair. One way or another, blood-washed or otherwise, the L.A. streets would be a lot cleaner on the morrow.

The petty officer in charge of the navy team grinned at Andy Foster and said, "Is this the guy they call The Executioner?"

"That's the guy," Foster replied sourly. "Can't you get a better fix?"

"This is RDF, you know, not radar," the sailor said. "We get an automatic triangulation every time we get a signal, but our receivers don't scramble out and identify each different voice that comes across. The only thing we can do is block track. You know—we can say, five minutes ago, they were all in the Beverly Hills area. At this moment they seem to be slightly south of Beverly Hills—but there's a fox out there, Lieutenant. I think it's the one they call Horse, and there is more than one voice involved, possibly two or three. He's running a diversion pattern and transmitting frequently, and we're getting no meaningful grouping on our fixes because of that. It will take at least another five minutes before we can identify a definite pullaway of the main group. Whoever this horse is, he damn well knows what he's about."

Another petty officer sitting close by removed a headset and joined the conversation. "I think I'm getting the same guy on Hardcase, too," he declared. "He's really screwing things up. Listen to this." He flipped a switch, throwing his monitor onto a loudspeaker.

"Zone Five Units, disregard last and stand by further," an officious voice commanded, on the Hardcase radio network.

"That's not your dispatcher," the navy man pointed out.

An exasperated voice blared in immediately to deny the validity of the previous announcement. A loud squeal immediately overrode that transmission, effectively blocking it. The navy men were grinning at each other.

"He's even jamming you," the leader told Foster.

"What can we do about it?" Foster demanded angrily.

The sailor shrugged. "You should have a contingency plan."

"Zone Six, Zone Six, disregard swirl and close on Alpha Three, that is Alpha Three, and stand by further."

"*That was not—*" Foster recognized it as Braddock's voice just before another ear-splitting squeal knocked him off the air.

The navy men were now laughing openly. Foster whirled to the intercom and shouted, "You've gotta get that damn horse!"

"Will you drop dead?" Braddock's tired voice came back.

Julian DiGeorge's massive Cadillac was eating up the Golden State Freeway. He was hunched over the wheel, heart pounding, mind whirling, and every snick of his tires seemed to be repeating, *idiot, idiot, idiot* . . . Deej had goofed—*oh* had he goofed! He had been so reluctant to return to the "old ways." Sure, sure, why not? Deep down in his

163

brain he must have known that there was no returning to old ways. Old ways are dead and gone; there's no way to get back to them. Deej had tried to step backward twenty years in one small step, and he'd just about landed in the grave of those dead old ways.

Times change, they change, and a guy has to change with the times. Sure, he knew that now. Try fighting a war nowadays using the same old weapons of the World War. Yeah, that's what Deej had done. Times had changed, war had changed, and Deej had tried to step back into the old ways. He'd thought he could scare Bolan off with a show of strength, and bastard Bolan had shoved that show right back through his teeth. Just a plain guy, huh? Plain hell!

Well, it was all lost now. The legitimacy, the respect, the comfortable floating with the cream of society—yeah, it was all gone now. The cops, the newspapers, the feds—everybody would start digging into the DiGeorge empire now. And the truth would out. Julian DiGeorge, *nee* Julio DiGeorgio, would be another name on the racket busters' lists. They'd investigate his banks, his ships, his politics—everything would get the big eye, and Deej would have to labor again. He would have to labor to his dying day.

Well—okay. Deej had always known, deep down, that he didn't really belong in the puking mass of social respectability. Deej was, by God, a laborer—and he wasn't ashamed of it. To hell with Beverly Hills. To hell with the bright boys with the phony smiles, and to hell with the hot tramps with the itching asses. To hell with it all. Deej was a laborer, and he was now headed for that laboring man's castle down in Balboa, the family home, a place where a man could stretch out and thumb his nose at the miserable cops and the puking social climbers and lunatics like soldier boy Bolan. Deej hoped Bolan would find Balboa. God, he hoped the miserable bastard would find it. He wouldn't find a bunch of foolish old idiots, trying to step into the past. No. Bolan would find the twentieth-century brotherhood at Balboa. He would find the Black Hand of God, by God, and in all its fury and potency.

"This is Horse, signing off, final transmission. Good luck, Sarge. Hope you win the war."

"Gadgets!" Bolan snapped. "Gadgets?"

Flower Andromede's calm tones came through. "Guess he can't hear you, Maestro. They're buzzed by the fuzz. No chance, no chance. I'm breaking. Scratch one politician and one ohms lawyer."

"Is it P.O.W., Flower?" Bolan inquired anxiously.

"Affirm. A quiet surrender. Where do you run? I'm rejoining."

Bolan's voice was heavy with a mixture of sadness and relief. "We run true. Your option, Flower. Head for the hutch if you'd rather."

"Neg. We're already three too few. I'll find you."

"I'm in clover," Zitka came in. "Are you on?"

"I'm on," Bolan assured him. "Guns? Where away?"

"Parallel to track and running true," Harrington reported.

"Roger. Guess we're clear. Keep running true."

"I couldn't hear Horse and Flower," Zitka complained. "What's happening?"

"The blues corralled the horse," Bolan replied. "Flower is rejoining, and just in time—it sounds like we're running beyond the radios."

"Maybe we broke outta the radio trap, then," Zitka observed soberly.

"Maybe so. But keep it minimum, just in case."

"Roj."

"Where do you run, Boom?"

"Closing on Gunsmoke right now," replied Hoff-ower's quiet voice.

"Okay. Let's try to tighten it up. Give me a fix, Zit, so I can verify track."

"I'm coming up on Victor Four," Zitka said.

"Mark your passage."

"Roj . . . stand by . . . mark."

"Okay. I am . . . two minutes light and closing. Let's all fall in now."

"I have you in my rear view, Maestro," Loudelk reported.

"Roger, I see you. Let's try to flock now. All birds, pull it in."

"Man I am flying in," Andromede's faint voice advised.

"There's still a straggling pip or two, but they seem to be heading down the Golden State," Foster reported excitedly. "And we're losing them fast."

"You'd think, with half the mobile units in town on the job, we could have plugged that damn . . ." Braddock fumed. He was reaching for his hat and stuffing things into his pockets. "Get my car ready! Extend the alert all the way to Oceanside and try to pull in Riverside, Redlands, Banning, San Jacinto, and anybody else you can get into that fan. Ask the CHP to seal Oceanside solid, and I mean *solid*."

"How far you figuring to chase these guys, Cap'n?" asked a uniformed officer.

"I'll chase 'em clear to Tijuana if I have to," Braddock roared.

The track ended a few miles above Balboa, on one of the irregular outjuttings of California coastline. They had left the interstate route some

minutes back to proceed along a twisting and tor-
turous blacktop road that swept down to the sea,
skirted a small inlet, then climbed several hundred
feet to the rocky promontory.

Bolan rolled to a halt behind Loudelk's vehicle.
Zitka's chase car, a little MG, was not in sight, but
Zitka himself was jogging quietly down the road
toward the clustering cars of the Death Squad. Bolan stepped out onto the ground just as another vehicle pulled up on his rear bumper. Loudelk had
slithered out to join Zitka; the two of them walked
on to Bolan's Porsche, where they were joined by
a grinning Gunsmoke Harrington. Washington
opened his door and stepped out, then leaned
across the roof of the Porsche with a sober smile.
A few scudding clouds were passing low overhead,
intermittently blocking out the faint nightlight.

Zitka had been busy lighting a cigarette. A stiff
coastal wind was making the job difficult. He
dragged hard on the cigarette and said, "End of
the line."

Bolan nodded. He was gazing out onto the long
promontory, mentally calculating the length,
breadth, and height. A large house at the far end
loomed grimly foreboding against the horizon.
Lights were showing faintly on all three floors of
the structure. "Is it sealed at this end?" he asked
Zitka.

"You better believe it. Stone wall, about ten feet
high, runs across the entire front. About a
hundred yards wide. Big iron gate right in the center. Brick gatehouse just inside. Maybe four guards
in there. I figure a thousand yards from the gate
down to the house. There's a guy walking the wall
with a shotgun."

"Conclusions?" Bolan asked tersely.

"It's a fortress."

Bolan nodded. "It figures. This is their hard site."

"Eighteenth-century mentality," Harrington put in.

"Maybe so," Bolan said, "but we have to figure a twentieth-century way to get in there."

Loudelk had walked to the far side of the road to gaze along the sheer drop to the ocean. "Almost straight up and down as far as I can see," he observed quietly. "And I'd hate to fall. Looks like nothing but rocks down below."

Bolan swung his gaze onto Harrington. "Wasn't Boom just behind you?"

"He's spotted back at the turnoff," Harrington yelled, "to make sure Flower doesn't get lost."

"I'm glad we have the benefit of Politician's last bright idea," Bolan said musingly. "Looks like we might need it."

"We going to bust on in?" Harrington inquired, smiling brightly.

"Might have to," Bolan replied. He turned to Zitka and Loudelk. "Give the place a thorough recon," he told the seasoned scouts. "Pay particular attention to the cliffs at the other side. Find a hold—any kind of hole."

Zitka and Loudelk exchanged glances, then slightly withdrew. Bolan watched them out of sight, then spoke into the radio. "Boom. Situation."

"Flower just arrived," Hoffower immediately responded. "On our way."

Bolan laid the radio on the hood of the Porsche and told the others, "Let's check the weapons."

Washington pulled the keys from the ignition and went to the rear and opened the trunk. Harrington was walking quickly to his vehicle, playing with the snapaway straps that held his six-shooters in place. Moments later, when the other vehicles joined them, an assortment of automatic weapons

168

and ammo clips were neatly arranged on the roof of the Porsche.

Hoffower was driving to a small panel truck and towing what appeared to be a low canvas-covered trailer. He pulled the rig even with the Porsche and immediately cut the motor. Andromede halted his vehicle, a late-model Fury, just to the rear.

Bolan gave them a brief rundown of the situation.

"Guess you're gonna need my tagalong, then," Hoffower observed.

Bolan jerked his head in a curt nod. "Pull on ahead of me, Boom, and get it unhitched. Give 'im a hand, Flower, and get that weapon ready to go. After you get unhitched, Boom, get your explosives ready. How many satchel charges do you have in there?"

"Six," Hoffower replied. "I can make a few more right quick if you think you need 'em."

Bolan shook his head. "Six should be enough. And break out four grenades for every man." He swiped at his nose and added in low tones, "Seven of us left—twenty-eight chunks, Boom."

Hoffower nodded, started his engine, and pulled off the road ahead of the Porsche. Andromede walked along beside the trailing vehicle, slashing at the ropes of the canvas with a knife. Washington stepped over to help him strip back the canvas and uncover the jeep. Hoffower was between the vehicles with a wrench, releasing the tow bar.

Andromede swung up behind the fifty-caliber mount, removed the dust cover, and busied himself with an ammo box.

Zitka and Loudelk materialized from the shadows along the road, and Zitka reported, "Not a hole anywhere, Mack. It's right up the middle or not at all."

Bolan had obviously been prepared for such a

finding. "Okay," he said. He spread his arms at shoulder height and waved both hands. "Gather 'round and let's go over the footwork. Time check first." He stared at his watch. "One-oh-seven ... right ... now. Boom, I want you to drape a satchel charge over the hood ornament of Zitka's vehicle. At precisely 1:15, Boom, you send that car against the gate. Give yourself plenty of room to drop clear. Flower, you on the fifty and Deadeye driving, right behind the battering ram. Hold back at about fifty feet and open up with that big mother. Rest of you deployed along the wall, and raise as much hell as you can without actually exposing yourself. Toss some grenades or something. Boom, I want four of those satchels. Now—nobody comes in. You're providing diversionary fire only, and I want you—"

"Just a damn minute!" Zitka protested. "You're going in there alone?"

"One man can do it, Zit," Bolan argued. "If you can pull everybody toward that gate, I can be over the wall and halfway to the house before anyone begins to wonder what's happening."

"With four damn satchel charges!" Harrington put in disgustedly.

"You're not leaving us standing around on the outside, Mack," Zitka said. "Look, we're all sorry about Chopper and about Pol and Gadgets. But we made the decision back at camp. We're going all the way."

"It's our war too, man," Deadeye Washington murmured.

"Boom?" Bolan queried, his eyes grim.

"Hell yes," Hoffower replied quietly. "This's no time to get faint."

"As a squad, we'll shoot our wad," Flower Child intoned.

Bolan's eyes dropped. When they came up
170

again, he was grinning. "Okay. We're still the Terrible Ten. Maybe Chopper's wild-ass charge was what sent all these bunnies hopping along the trail. His effect is right here with us. Pol and Gadgets provided the police diversion that got us here. So . . ."

"So the squad's all present and accounted for," Andromede said. "Now let's go show those cats what a firefight looks like."

"Deal the cards again, Sarge," Harrington said.

"Okay. We still use the satchel on the MG, but Zitka drives. It'll give just as much punch on that gate as any tank, and it's light enough to be moved out of the way. Flower, Deadeye, and Gunsmoke in the jeep. Swing wide just outside and provide covering fire while we clear that gateway. Boom, use your truck and ram right on through. Try to push the MG inside and out of the way. If you still have wheels under you then, stand by to fall in on the procession. If not, get clear and join the first vehicle you can.

"Deadeye, swing that jeep in right behind Boom's truck but wait until the way is clear. Flower, after penetrating the gate, keep your fire to the left of the road and fire at anything that moves or looks like it could move. Gunsmoke, I want you in the front, beside Deadeye. Get your big chopper—you're sweeping the right side and the road ahead. Bloodbrother, you fall in behind the jeep. Pick up Zitka and punch right on in. I'll bring up the rear in the Porsche. Boom, you better just plan on leaving the truck and joining me. I'll need a rear gunner.

Now this will be a punch in, pure and simple. No telling how many active troops we'll be leaving behind us. We'll have to punch right back out again probably, and if the blues show, we're going to be in a hell of a tight situation. So let's keep it

171

fast and furious, and the sooner we get moving the better.

"Let's get everything out of the truck and into the punch vehicles. Let's get moving, let's go go go!"

Sergeant Carl Lyons slowed his car to a leisurely pace and snatched up his hand mike. "CHP says no movement into Balboa, Captain," he reported. "I just passed a road running off toward the cliffs. Think I'll investigate."

"I'm only a couple minutes behind you now," Braddock's unhappy tones came back at him. "Wait for us there."

"Ten-four." Lyons threw down the mike and swerved abruptly across the median in a fishtailing U-turn, then powered into the northbound lanes. A moment later he was leaning into a curving exit and passing beneath the highway in an easy glide toward the beach. Over in the darkness he could detect a rugged point of land rising to the horizon. He braked to a halt and swiveled about in the seat for a view of the highway, then spoke again into the microphone. "Right where the highway breaks slightly inland into the hills," he directed. "A small cove to the right, narrow blacktop leading down."

"Okay," Braddock replied.

Lyons was gazing toward the promontory. Faint lights shone over there, on the far end of the outcropping. Then a bright flame shot up high into the air, toward the beginning of the promontory, and an instant later the explosive roar reached Lyons's ears. He was already stepping on the accelerator as he told Braddock, "Paydirt! You can't miss it now! Just follow the flames!"

Zitka leaped from the speeding MG and hit the

ground in a tight roll. A man ran out of the gate-house just as the careening vehicle smashed into the steel gate with an instantaneous clap of thunder and whooshing flames. The jeep swung in a tight arc past Zitka as he scrambled to his feet and sprinted back down the road. The deep rattle of the big fifty mingled with the secondary explosion of the MG's gas tank and the excited cries coming from beyond the flames.

Harrington raised his gun to track onto a man who was running along the wall; the gun burped briefly, and the running man disappeared beyond the wall.

The panel truck swerved around the curve and cautiously approached the flaming wreckage in the gateway; then gears meshed, and the deep whine of low gear propelled the truck into the crackling pile. Harrington had scrambled out of the jeep and was standing against the wall, his gun chattering, to cover the maneuver. The truck whined on through the debris, pushing it along in a grinding scream of protesting metal, while the jeep circled about and fell in to the rear. Harrington leaped aboard and remained standing in the front floor, his weapon raking the gatehouse in an incessant sweeping. Men were running and shouting, and the sound of gunfire issued from deeper inside the grounds. The windshield of the jeep shattered, and Harrington abruptly sat down.

Two men stood behind the gatehouse, firing at the truck with revolvers. They crumpled and jerked to the ground under the heavy staccato of the fifty caliber. Flames were shooting from the hood of the truck as Hoffower flung the door open and bailed out. The jeep moved swiftly along the narrow drive. Loudelk's sedan spurted through the gateway and quickly closed on the jeep; then Bolan's Porsche roared in. Hoffower had darted across the drive and was kneeling in the grass, his .45 spitting flame toward the wall. The Porsche slowed momentarily, and the door swung open; Hoffower jumped in and slammed the door, and they spun out with a shriek of rubber.

The jeep was leading the fast-moving procession, its automatic weapons rattling angrily. Tracers were leaping out from the big fifty, probing the terrain ahead. Shouts and curses could be heard on both sides, rising above the explosive reports of gunfire.

If Beverly Hills had boasted a company, Bolan was thinking, this place easily supported a battalion. The window just behind his head shattered. Hoffower immediately announced, "I'm hit," in a quiet voice. He swiveled in the seat and pushed the .45 out the window in his left hand and began firing at running, shadowy figures on their right flank. Bolan risked a glance at his partner. A red groove traversed one side of his face, oozing blood.

"Grazed," Hoffower amended as he ejected a spent clip and snapped in a replacement.

The jeep was now running about, broadside to Bolan's travel, and the fifty was tracering up Bolan's left flank. They had reached the circular portion of the drive, in front of the house. Bolan swung in behind the sedan just as Loudelk and Zitka bolted from the vehicle. Flame was spitting at them from several basement windows, and Harrington's chopper was replying. The death squad was caught in a cross fire, with enemy reinforcements gathering quickly to both sides of their soft position.

"Take the house!" Bolan cried.

Loudelk and Zitka sprinted to opposite corners of the house, grenades in their hands. Bolan stepped to the ground with a chopper in one hand and a satchel charge in the other. He twirled the

174

charge overhead, then let it fly. It hit the massive doors at the front of the house with a deafening roar, and licking flames immediately brightened the landscape. Bolan tossed another charge into French doors on the second floor, and the explosion blended with lesser ones coming simultaneously from the sides of the house.

Harrington was dueling with enemy fire from both floors and the basement; Andromede was checking the advance on their rear with the big fifty. Deadeye Washington had snatched up a chattergun and was making a run for the front door. A burst of fire from an upstairs window caught him full in the chest, and the big fellow went to ground with his weapon chattering. Bolan, also in motion toward the door, had to spin past Washington's falling body. A pain shot up from his heel, and he realized that he was hit also, but he was up the steps and charging through the flaming doorway with Harrington pushing close behind, and the heel was forgotten. He charged into a large room just as a clump of men were descending a circular stairway. Bolan chopped at them; two fell, and three more raced back up the stairs.

Harrington's burper was swinging toward an arched doorway at the rear, and another two men were flung to the floor. The burper went silent; Harrington shook it, then tossed it aside and released the straps of his six-guns as he moved swiftly toward the stairway.

Bolan glanced at him and snapped, "The basement!"

Harrington nodded and swung back to Bolan's side. The house was burning, the flames beginning to roar on the top floor. They found the basement stairs in an alcove beyond the main room, just as a pair of men ran into the house through the front door. Harrington said, "I'll cover!" and stepped out with both guns blazing. Bolan wondered vaguely about the other four of his squad and about the fact that two enemy had managed to get inside, but there was no time for speculation. He was already halfway through the doorway to the basement stairs.

He dodged back as a bullet thwacked into the wood alongside his head, then leaned around the curve and dropped a grenade over the staircase. He followed the explosion with a headlong plunge down the stairs, sweeping indiscriminately with the chopper. There was no return fire. A bookcase along one wall burst into flame, eerily lighting the underground scene. Dead bodies were flung about, and nothing moved. At the bottom of the stairs lay a man who Bolan had watched earlier that night through his sniperscope. Deadeye had said, "That's Varone there, the little one."

Bolan swung back up the stairway and erupted into the alcove. Gunsmoke Harrington lay there on his back, his chest wetly red and his lips flecked with red foam. "Look out, Sarge," he said faintly, and died.

A white-haired man loomed up in Bolan's side vision. A shotgun roared just as Bolan flung himself toward the corner. Bolan felt the sting of several straggling pellets, and he knew that the main charge had missed him. He was twisting about to bring the chopper up, when DiGeorge flung the shotgun at him and darted for the front door. The discarded gun flanged against Bolan's weapon and diverted his aim. He scrambled to his feet and gave chase, reaching the steps just as the whine of police sirens bored in on his consciousness.

The house was engulfed in flames now. Bolan staggered down the steps, his mind numbed, and

176

walked stiffly through incredible carnage. Bodies littered the drive in front of the house, and there was no movement anywhere Bolan could see. He gazed down at the grotesquely curled caricature of what had once been Deadeye Washington. Several yards away lay the remains of Boom-Boom Hoffower. Flower Child Andromede was crumped atop the fifty.

Bolan threw back his head and yelled, "Zitter! Brother! *Regroup!*" The sirens were screaming up the blacktop—almost to the gate, Bolan figured. He jogged around the corner of the house and immediately found Zitka. The fierce little fighter was clutching a machine pistol and snarling, even in death.

Bolan found Bloodbrother Loudelk at the rear. Half of his head was missing. Otherwise, he looked very peaceful. In life, Bolan thought, so in death. He wearily returned to the Porsche, wondering where all the enemy had gone, and tossed the chopper onto the rear deck, then slumped into the seat. He was sealed in, and the rest of the squad was dead. Who the hell cared about the enemy? What a hell of a mess he had made of things. They should have aborted. They should, at least, have lain back and figured out some better way to make this strike.

The sirens were swinging through the gates now, starting the short journey down the promontory. Bolan started the Porsche and wheeled it around into the grass. His heel hurt like hell, and he was slowly discovering other nicks and scrapes in tender places. He gunned away from the sirens and drew up at the low wooden railing that marked the end of land, then got out and unhurriedly studied the drop to the ocean below. Bloodbrother had been right; it looked like nothing but rocks below. No chance of diving for it—he'd never clear those rocks. Unless . . .

Bolan got back into the Porsche, securely fastened the safety belt, and gunned back to the driveway. He could see the flashing bubble-gum machines on top of their cars now. Quite a parade. He sighed. The Death Squad was a dead squad now. He'd offered them wealth and glory and given them only death in a war that nobody cheered for. Like 'Nam. Yeah, just like 'Nam.

He double-checked the safety belt, then screamed around in a wild U-turn, straightening out into a full-power run toward the wooden railing. His tires slipped a bit on the damp grass, but the needle kept climbing in a steady movement toward the end of the speedometer. He flipped a glance into the rear-view mirror. The parade had arrived at the front of the house, and bluesuits with riot guns were pouring out everywhere. A lone vehicle was tearing on after the Porsche.

The needle was vibrating at 120 when he felt the slight resistance of the flimsy barrier, and then he was floating free, arcing out into a beautiful dive over the blue Pacific. "Roll call," he muttered. The entire squad was sitting there with him; they had all brought him here, each one, through gallantry above and beyond the call. And he was taking them with him, in effect anyway, in this final, desperate, gallant fling through this hell called life.

Chapter Sixteen

THE REVERSE WALK

Carl Lyons had left his car at the blacktop and walked down to the water's edge. He stood there with his hands in his pockets, rocking gently on the balls of his feet. If *he'd* been in that hurtling vehicle, Lyons reasoned, and if he'd been still alive when the thing settled into the water, and if he'd managed to get out of it, and if he'd had the strength and the guts and the determination to try swimming to freedom—then this would be the spot he would be trying for. Not that there was much chance of Bolan's swimming away from *that* plunge. Just the same . . . The coast-guard boat had responded promptly, and they were even now preparing to send divers down. *If* and *when* they came up with a body, then and only then would Carl Lyons believe that Bolan was dead.

A soft sound behind him spun him around, and the sergeant found himself gazing into the bore of a .38 police special. The gun was in the hand of Lieutenant Charlie Rickert, and the eyes behind the gun looked anything but sane, even in the muted nightlight.

"What're you doing here, Rickert?" Lyons asked calmly.

"You and Bolan didn't really think you could pull it off, did you?" Rickert sneered. "On the twenty-four-hour cop? You didn't actually think you'd make it stick, did you?"

"What are you talking about?"

"Get your hands behind your head! What the hell you think? You know damn well what I'm talking about. You and Bolan cooked this thing up.

179

Did you think I'd hold still for that kind of crap, Lyons?" Rickert laughed, a dry, rattling sound. "You thought Charlie Rickert couldn't find out. Look, wet-behind-the-ears, I was a cop while you was still sucking tit."

"What are you hoping to accomplish, Rickert?" Lyons was slowly shifting to one side, trying to maneuver his new adversary into a better light.

"Just stand still!" Rickert snarled.

"How long have you been a bad cop, Rickert?"

"I'm going to kill you, youngster. You know that, don't you?"

"Why, Rickert?" Lyons had detected a flicker of motion in the shadows behind Rickert. He kept the conversation going and again began a slow movement toward the water. "What do you have to gain? Braddock has all the evidence he needs. He's already signed your suspension. A full-scale investigation will start tomorrow."

"No, no, no. All they have is contrived evidence, put together by a mass murderer and his cop accomplice."

"What ever gave you the idea that I've been working with Bolan, Rickert?"

"Charlie Rickert has his ways, and Charlie Rickert knows all. Don't you worry how I found out. You're a lousy cop, Lyons. You can't even spot a tail. I been on you all night."

"Just waiting for a chance like this, eh?"

"That's right. Just waiting for a chance . . . just . . . like . . . *this!*" Rickert had thrust the .38 forward and was squeezing down on the trigger, when the shadow behind him came alive. A hand chopped down on his gun arm, and an elbow burrowed into his gut as the gun was falling. The shadow whirled, a fist arched out and splattered into Rickert's face, and he went down without a sound.

180

A hand quickly scooped up the fallen .38, and a familiar voice said, "We're always meeting."

Lyons stared at the tall, dripping figure in the black suit. "How long you been standing behind that rock, Bolan?" he asked.

"Long enough to get my breath," Bolan replied, still panting slightly.

"Then you heard the gist of that conversation?"

"I heard it."

"You knew he was about to gun me down. Why didn't you wait another second? Then you could have chopped him and had a clear field."

Bolan shrugged. "I couldn't bug off and leave Tommy to solve that problem alone."

"What?"

"You know. The moles."

Lyons chuckled. "I've been doing some reading on lawn pests, Bolan. They're destructive, yeah, but they serve a useful purpose too. This book tells me I shouldn't be too quick to cut down on the moles. Guess I'll try a bit of peaceful coexistence."

"You trying to delay me, Lyons? The way you did Rickert?" Bolan was beginning to move slowly away.

"Not at all. Uh, Bolan. Some dumb cop left his car unprotected up there on the road. Keys in it and everything."

"Yeah?"

"Yeah." Lyons knelt beside Rickert and snapped a pair of cuffs on him. "He'll keep for a while. And now that same dumb cop is going to take a walk among the rocks, hoping to find a survivor from that car plunge off the cliff over there. Uh, happy coexistence, Bolan. This time *I'm* walking." Lyons turned abruptly and strode off into the darkness.

Bolan smiled tightly and moved quickly toward the road. Life wasn't *all* hell, he decided. Another battle had ended. Perhaps somewhere, someday, he would find a place to end the war. Flower had been wrong. Hell was not for the living, it was for the dead, even the hallowed dead. Let the dead rest in peace. Someday Mack Bolan, too, would rest. For now, he had to find his way among the living. And he would find Julian DiGeorge somewhere about that landscape, and undoubtedly many more just like him.

He would never, however, find another Death Squad. Not like the helluva bunch he'd just lost. He climbed behind the wheel of Lyons's vehicle, started the engine, and moved slowly out. His glance fell on the microphone.

"Roll Call," he said, half-aloud.

And he could have sworn he heard them checking in. Bloodbrother, Zitter, Gunsmoke, Deadeye, Boom-Boom, Flower Child, Chopper, Gadgets, and Politician. They were all in—and they were all on Mack Bolan.